DEATH WALK
by
Walt Morey

Blue Heron Publishing, Inc.
Hillsboro, Oregon

DEATH WALK

Published by

Blue Heron Publishing, Inc.
24450 NW Hansen Road
Hillsboro, Oregon 97124
503.621.3911

ISBN: 0-936085-18-5 (cloth)
ISBN: 0-936085-55-X (paper)

Library of Congress Catalog Card Number: 91-70157

Printed in the United States of America

First trade paperback edition
10 9 8 7 6 5 4 3 2 1

To the women in my life —
Peggy and Lucy,
my wife and my daughter

Other Books by Walt Morey
presently in the Walt Morey Adventure Library

Gloomy Gus

•

Runaway Stallion

•

Scrub Dog of Alaska

•

Year of the Black Pony

•

Angry Waters

•

Run Far, Run Fast

•

Home is the North

•

Deep Trouble

•

Death Walk (cloth)

- 1 -

I rolled onto my back. I could see the black pattern of trees and, beyond, the glacial blue of the northern sky. Silence engulfed me. Silence like you might find at the bottom of a well — or in death. Something terrible had happened, but my numbed mind refused to grapple with it.

Certain things came through. The ground was spongy beneath me. There was a needle-sharp coldness against my cheeks. I tested my arms and legs. They were stiff, but they moved okay. My head throbbed. I raised a hand and felt a tender lump. I explored it with careful fingers. There was no blood.

I sat up and looked about. The earth was blanketed with snow. But how could that be? There was no snow where I lived just outside Seattle.

Then I realized I was wearing an Eskimo parka. I was wearing Eskimo mukluks. Where were my shoes?

I looked around trying to bring logic to this crazy predicament. I was surrounded by torn-up snow. There was a huge snow-covered rock near me with an overturned snowmobile leaning against it. All about me were clothes, cans of food, an axe, sleeping bag, and pieces of fiberglass from the wrecked machine.

I tried to stand. Dizziness overcame me and nausea rose in my throat. I lay down again, pulled the parka hood close around my face, and tried to think. But so great was the pain, nothing came.

I turned my head carefully, my eyes surveying the situation. I scooped up a handful of snow, rubbed it hard across my face, and looked again. I concentrated on the dark shape of the snowmobile. Then, like a curtain pulled aside, it all came back to me with a rush.

My good friend, Ross Edwards, was dead. Killed by someone back at a trapper's cabin. I'd been trying to escape. We'd flown somewhere in Alaska to bring snowmobile fuel and other supplies to the trapper before winter closed in. When we landed, no one was there to meet us. There was no sign of the man who'd radioed for Ross to come. We'd begun unloading the plane, figuring the man would return any minute.

I was in the lean-to behind the cabin putting the containers of gasoline for the trapper's snowmobile under the tarp that covered the machine. Ross was in the plane gathering the final load. There was a sharp crack. The sound of a rifle, I thought. I looked around the corner of the cabin in time to see a second shot disintegrate the plane's windshield. Ross was pinned down inside the cockpit, even if he hadn't been hit. I ducked out of sight. More shots came from somewhere in the line of trees beyond the icy meadow where we'd landed. They slammed into the fuselage of the plane. The sound sent tremors of terror up my spine. Then I heard the explosion. I knew the worst had happened. Whoever was shooting had hit the aircraft's fuel tank.

My friend was dead. How would I return home? I crawled into a gap between the woodpile and the cabin wall and hid. I wanted to cry but I was afraid to make a sound. I huddled there, fearing that at any moment I'd be discovered.

It seemed like hours, but was probably only minutes, before I heard footsteps inside the cabin. Then the door closed and there was silence. I expected someone to look behind the building. I kept listening for the crunch of boots on the crusty snow. No one came. I waited until the cold had stiffened me before I crawled carefully out and peeked around the corner. The only thing visible was the twisted, smoldering wreckage of the plane. A plume of black smoke rose lazily into the calm sky. I leaned against the woodpile and let my tears come. I was alone and more frightened than ever in my life.

By the time approaching dusk cloaked the cabin in shadows I was through feeling sorry for myself. I mourned for Ross, but I knew it was up to me if I was going to survive. I began to think of how I might escape.

I let myself into the cabin but didn't light any of the kerosene lamps for fear the killer still lurked outside watching. For the same reason, I couldn't build a fire to shake the terrible chill that penetrated to my bones. A chill that was caused by more than just the icy cold of the North. In the dim light that still seeped through the small windows and the open door, I searched through the cabin for anything that might help. I looked for the radio that had called Ross in. It was nowhere to be found, though the antenna wires hung limply down the wall above the table.

I realized that whoever had murdered Ross might also have killed the trapper. We must have interrupted his leisurely looting. I knew I had to hurry before the killer returned. He'd surely be back for the supplies we'd brought. A sleeping bag and pack were in one corner. I grabbed both and stuffed the pack with a change of clothes from the trapper's shelf. I pulled on a pair of heavy, loose trousers over my jeans. A pair of mukluks next to the bed were too big, but with an extra pair of wool socks they fit fine. I filled a duffel bag with food, pocketed a box of wooden matches, and took the axe leaning next to the stove. I donned a parka and mittens before lugging my load to the lean-to. The last thing I took was a map tacked to the wall.

I wrapped everything tightly in the tarp and tied it to the back of the snowmobile. The key was in the machine. I turned it and heard the motor crank coldly but it wouldn't catch. I was about to panic when I realized that it must be out of gas. And that was why the killer hadn't taken it before. I filled the tank and strapped two five gallon cans to the load. I'd nearly forgotten them in my rush.

This time the motor came to life. The din it made was sure to carry for miles, I thought, but I had no choice. Besides, I'd be out of there and moving fast before anyone could respond. The problem was which way to go. I remembered that Ross had flown into the place over the low hills still silhouetted by the dying sun. West, then, until I was safely away. Tomorrow I could study the map and figure a way out.

The snowmobile was powerful and it took me some time to get the hang of steering it safely. I wanted to hurry, but when I sped up it was like riding a bucking horse. It didn't take long to reach the hills, but by then it was really dark. I guided the machine carefully through the trees. Finally, I crested the ridge and started down the other side. It had clouded over and a light powdery snow was falling.

I felt safer with my tracks being covered, but I wanted to put more distance between me and the cabin before I stopped. When I reached the bottom of the hills, I was on another flat like the one where we'd landed. I felt more confident in speeding up, despite the snowy darkness. But without landmarks I had no idea how far I'd come. I didn't even know if I was still heading west. Finally, the flat terrain gave way to rolling hills with some trees. I'd been gone from the cabin for nearly three hours. I thought it would be safe to find shelter and wait for morning. No sense wasting gas going the wrong direction. That's when it happened.

The flying snowmobile hit something, shot into the air, twisted end over end, and slammed head on into the rock. I must have been knocked out for hours. Now it was light again. The snow had stopped long ago. Only a light dusting covered the scattered gear. I could still see my backtracks leading up to the rock. I struggled to my feet to check the damage to the machine. My right leg caved in with such a savage stab of pain I collapsed on my face. I rolled over, sat up and grabbed my ankle with both hands. The pain came with driving force and raced the length of my leg.

I gingerly felt my ankle and tried to move it. The pain was so great I was sure it was broken. I rolled over on my stomach and crawled the thirty or so feet to the snowmobile, dragging my right leg. One close look told me the whole story: the runners on the front were hopelessly smashed. I wrapped my arms around myself and began to shake, and a great loss went crying through me. I tried not to think.

A rabbit hopped nearby and disappeared behind a snowy hummock. A great white owl planed silently out of the sky, talons

4

spread. Behind the hummock there was a single terrified squeal, then the owl flapped heavily aloft, the rabbit in its talons.

There was silence then. Silence broken by a series of high, savage cries, bloodcurdling and fearsome. They echoed and reached far back amongst the forbidding peaks, then faded away like the wild notes of an organ. I had never heard the howl of a wolf pack, but I instinctively knew this was the voice of a pack hot on the trail of some unfortunate animal.

I sat there a long time. The cold started to eat into me and finally I began to think of myself and my predicament. I couldn't stay here. The only cabin I knew of was the one I'd left last night. That was now many miles and a range of hills behind me. It was also the last place I wanted to go. With this broken ankle, I couldn't walk any distance. I was achingly, fearfully alone in a strange and empty land. No one would search No one knew I was here.

Freezing, I'd heard, wasn't painful. You just became sort of numb and went to sleep. I was surprised I could think about it so calmly. Maybe because I couldn't really believe it would happen.

I pulled the map from my pocket and began to plan what I could do. The trapper had marked the position of his cabin with a red circle. If I'd kept traveling west before the accident, I was probably thirty or forty miles in the general direction of another spot marked on the map. The name Jake was penciled beside it, so I figured it was another trapper's cabin. There was plenty of canned food lying about. But I couldn't carry enough for the days it would take to travel that fifty or so miles. And how would I travel? Crawl? But I couldn't crawl fifty miles! Maybe I'd meet another trapper. Perhaps, when Ross was missed, search planes would follow his flight plan to the cabin. They'd come right over-head. I stopped thinking how impossible it was. I had to try to crawl out. There was nothing else to do.

I got the pack and crawled about stuffing cans of food into it. I lashed the axe and sleeping bag to the pack frame, and, sitting up, managed to get the load securely on my back. Finally I was ready to go. I looked once more at the broken snowmobile and wondered for the hundredth time if there was a way to fix it. But

I knew there wasn't. I looked at the sun's feeble glow behind the overcast, trying to get my bearings. That's when I realized that I'd been heading north when I slammed into the rock. How long I had been riding in the wrong direction I didn't know. But one thing I knew for sure: I now had no idea where I was. Dragging my damaged ankle, I started to crawl away toward the trees to the west.

It was heartbreakingly slow and painful crawling through a foot of snow. I made a couple of hundred yards, then the pain in my ankle forced me to stop and rest. I had a small pocket knife and thought of cutting the mukluk off so I could see the damage. But I doubted I could get the mukluk on again over the swollen ankle, and I'd ruin it and my foot would surely freeze.

I was getting ready to begin crawling again when I had the uncomfortable feeling eyes were watching me. I looked up and there they were. How long they'd been standing there I'd no idea.

Wolves! A pair of them, and no more than fifty feet away. My mouth was suddenly cotton dry. My heart gave a thunderous leap and began hammering madly. They were the first live ones I'd ever seen. One was gray, smaller, the other was a big, black, ugly-looking brute, with the biggest teeth I'd ever seen in a dog-like animal.

I tried to get up, but I got only to my knees and the stabbing pain in my ankle stopped me. I looked wildly about for something, anything to defend myself with. I remembered the axe. I slipped out of the pack and pulled it free. I waved it menacingly and shouted at the top of my lungs, "Beat it! Get out of here! Go on, beat it!"

The gray one, I guessed it was a female, cocked her head and looked at me. The black one's eyes drilled into me with a look that sent chills racing up my back. Then he lowered his head, still staring straight at me. I had the feeling he'd made up his mind about something. He began leisurely walking toward me through the snow, his big head down, his eyes unwavering. I felt he was deliberately measuring me for a lightening attack.

For one horrible instant panic tore through me. A throat-tearing scream readied itself in my chest. I wanted to cry hysteri-

6

cally. But some cool part of my mind said it would be useless. I had to meet this animal and do it alone. When the wolf closed on me I had to use the axe. Maybe I could hit him, or hold him and his mate at bay.

An odd thought flitted through my mind. Yesterday, when Ross had been killed, and earlier today when I'd realized my predicament, I thought I'd experienced fear. That had been only dread. Now I was facing raw, tooth-rattling terror.

The wolf was not halfway to me when a shot tore the morning silence. A geyser of snow spurted up under the his nose. He bounded into the air startled. A voice shouted, "Go on, Blackie. Get!" The wolf whirled and with the gray following disappeared into the trees.

A man came wading through the snow carrying a rifle. He stopped at the overturned snowmobile, looked at it closely, then came on. I was sure this was the man who'd killed Ross. He must have followed my tracks all night. Now he would finish me.

He looked like a shaggy giant in his loose-fitting parka and mukluks. He might have been an inch or so shorter than my father, but there was a big, lean man under those loose-fitting northern clothes. He pushed back the parka hood. His hair was black, shoulder length, and hung in two braids down the sides of his face. His face was craggy, bony, his chin broad, blunt. I held the axe ready as he approached.

When he got closer, I could see his sharp, brown eyes. He carried a heavy rifle in one hand. His voice was deep, even. It fit the size of him. "How you doing, kid?"

"All right," I croaked. The relief at not being instantly shot almost overwhelmed me. This must not be the murderer, I thought. I'd been found.

"You can lay that axe aside. I won't do you any harm. Are you hurt any place special?"

"My ankle seems to be broken. I can't put any weight on it and it's swollen."

"Get your foot out here, let's see." He helped pull the mukluk off and felt my ankle, worked it gently back and forth, and said, "I doubt it's broken. My guess is you've got a bad sprain, which can hurt as bad as a break, but which you'll get over in a couple of days. You're lucky. The nearest doctor is two hundred miles. For what you've been through you seem in good shape, better than the snowmobile."

"Yes," I said.

"You've got a couple of black eyes," he ran on, "a cut lip, a big bump over the eyebrow, and one smack in the middle of your forehead. If you hadn't been in this crack-up I'd say you were in a fight."

"I was," I said.

"You win?"

"No."

"Well," he said soberly, "you win some. You lose some. Just what happened here? Where were you going? Where'd you come from? How'd you get here? I want it all."

"We came from Seattle. We were taking stuff up to a trapper."

"I know of no other trapper near here. And who is 'we'?"

"Ross, my friend. Someone destroyed our plane with him in it. He's dead. And I don't know where the cabin is anymore. I traveled about three hours last night. I think it's over those hills somewhere." I pointed at the far distant ridge.

"A three hour run. That could be fifty or sixty miles, depending on your speed, which by the looks of things was pretty fast. You flew up from Seattle, you say? And what's this about someone killing your partner? You'd better explain yourself better than that. Murder's a serious charge."

I wanted to tell this man the whole story, but I didn't know who he was. His silence outwaited my reluctance. Finally, I sketched what had happened. He listened without comment, watching my face closely as I let my story pour out. When I'd finished, I asked, "How'd you find me?"

"By accident. I crossed your trail back a ways. Your tracks were weaving all over so I figured something was wrong. Besides, nobody should be out here now. So I tracked you and found you." He took a hand axe from his belt and said, "You sit tight. I'll cut a couple of limbs for crutches so you can walk."

"Where are you taking me?" I asked.

"My cabin, about three miles north."

"I can't walk that far through this snow or crutches," I protested.

"You were crawlin' on hands and knees. How far'd you expect to get? Get one thing straight, I'm not carryin' you."

"But three miles," I insisted. "In this weather?"

"In this weather," he said, and walked off.

I sat in the snow holding my aching ankle and listened to the chopping in the distant trees. Soon he was back with two cut limbs, trimmed and lopped off at the crotch. He helped me stand and I put one under each arm using the crotch for the arm rest. He shouldered my pack and said, "All right, let's go."

All this time, the two wolves had been sitting a short way off watching us. I said, "You're not going to kill those wolves? They were going to eat me."

"Wolves don't like human flesh." He turned and started off.

I was determined he should be more concerned. "But they're wolves," I insisted.

"So?" he asked with maddening calm.

"They ought to be killed."

"Kid, you've got an awful lot to learn."

I had to swing the crutches hard and fast to keep up. I made probably a quarter of a mile, then I yelled that I had to rest and sat down on a frozen hummock. He gave me about five minutes, then said, "Let's go. You're soft as mush."

The same two wolves appeared about a hundred yards to our right. The man saw them because he turned his head. But he did nothing.

When I thought they'd left they popped out some fifty yards ahead of us. I couldn't understand why the man didn't shoot them. He was obviously a trapper and their hides were worth something, and there was also the bounty. But he plodded ahead as if there wasn't a wolf in a hundred miles.

We had worn out the short northern daylight hours before we reached the cabin. Once the daylight was gone the wolves seemed to come closer. They were silent, slithering shadows against the white snow. They followed almost to the cabin door.

The cabin stood in the open against a backdrop of snow-laden trees. It was like the one I'd been at with Ross — small, oblong, and built of weather-beaten logs. A tin chimney stuck through the foot of snow on the roof. Stovewood was piled along one side. On the other side was a small cabin about six feet square built on poles high in the air — his cache, where the meat was kept frozen by the weather. A ladder provided the only access.

With the man's help I hobbled inside and sat down on the single wooden bench. He lit an oil lamp that hung from the ceiling, then got a fire going.

There was a rough table, the bench I sat on, and a wood stove in the corner. Pots and pans lined a high shelf on the wall. Here and there, pegs were driven into the logs for a variety of rough clothing and gear.

In a surprisingly short time the room was warm and the man had a meal on the table consisting of biscuits, moose steak, beans, and coffee. He ate in silence, only glancing at me occasionally and frowning. At the moment I wasn't interested in conversation. I was ravenously hungry and I'd never tasted lighter biscuits. I told him so.

"You'll be getting a lot of them," he said and was quiet again.

Supper over, he cleared a stack of boxes from a second bunk and unrolled my sleeping bag on it. I hobbled over and lay down. The ankle pain was coming through strong. Every throb brought back painful images of Ross caught in the burning plane.

The man filled a pan with snow and put it on the stove. When it melted he added more snow to cool the water and put it on the floor beside the bunk. "We'll start out as if this was just a bad sprain," he explained. "Put your foot in there. Cold water will help take down the swelling and ease the pain." His voice remained impersonal, matter-of-fact. There seemed to be no human warmth in him.

But he was right. The pain melted away to a dull ache. And now with my full stomach and the warm room, I was getting drowsy.

The man sat down on the bench facing me and said, "All right, let's do a little talking. I'm Mike Donovan. Who're you?"

"Joel Rogers, but I go by Joe," I mumbled. The heat and the food and the reaction to the day's happenings were getting to me. My eyes were weighted with lead. My voice sounded far away. "Joe Rogers," I mumbled again.

Donovan's voice said after a moment, "Guess you've been through too much to talk tonight, but we need to get this murder stuff sorted out as soon as possible. We'll postpone this talk until tomorrow."

I think I said, "Okay."

Tired as I was, one thing came through very clear. Here in this rough little log cabin, with this big, somber, tough-looking man scowling down at me, was the end of my tragic headlong flight into the trackless, frozen North.

- 2 -

Donovan was gone when I awoke. The cabin was getting cold but there were coals in the firebox.

The swelling was almost gone from my ankle. I got off the bunk and put weight on it. It wouldn't take my full weight, but I could hobble. I filled the stove and hunted for something to eat. There was an open bowl with batter and a slab of bacon on a shelf. I cut two strips and made pancakes for breakfast. Afterward I soaked my foot again in cold water. By noon I could move about reasonably well. The wood in the box was low. I got into my parka to go outside for more. The moment I opened the door I saw the wolves.

They were the two that had come after me and had followed us to the cabin. They sat on their tails looking at me. I held the door open, ready to step back and slam it against an attack.

The black one dropped his head and gave me that measuring stare, as unafraid as he'd been yesterday. Again it raised the hair on the back of my neck and a small fear chased through me. The gray one studied me, sharp ears pricked forward. Her tail waved slightly, she cocked her head, curious, not menacing. I yelled and made throwing motions, "Get out of here, beat it!" The gray one half turned, ready to run. The black stood his ground. I backed into the cabin and closed the door.

There was a rifle leaning in a corner, but it was empty. I searched for shells. Donovan might not kill these wolves, but I would. There were no shells. It was just as well. I'd never shot a rifle or any other gun. The wood in the box would have to last until Donovan returned or the wolves left. I had no intention of venturing outside with that black brute waiting.

I peeked out every few minutes but they still sat looking toward the cabin. I fed the stove a stick at a time to keep some fire going and held back most of the cold. But the cabin gradually turned chilly, so I checked the few sticks in the box and rationed them even more slowly.

The wood ran out and the wolves still waited. I tried to look through the window and gauge the approaching dusk, but the frost on the glass was an inch thick. I hobbled to the door often but the wolves were there. The northern twilight seeped off the distant ridges and flowed over the tundra and cabin.

The last stick of wood burned down to coals. I lit the lamp and slipped into my parka to keep warm.

I was trying not to shiver when the door opened and Donovan came in. Behind him I glimpsed a sled fastened with ropes for pulling and piled with the gear I'd abandoned with the snowmobile. "Holy smoke!" he said, "You let the fire go out."

"I tried to go for wood," I said, "but those wolves have been waiting out there for hours. They're the same ones that tried to get me yesterday — and followed us to the cabin. I'd have killed them, but there's no shells for that rifle in the corner. I looked everywhere."

"You leave those wolves alone," he said sharply.

"But they're wolves — they're dangerous. I've read a lot about wolves."

"I'll bet you have — written by amateurs and know-it-alls," Donovan said disgustedly. "You've never been ten feet from a fire plug in your life." He went outside and a couple of minutes later returned with a frozen slab of moose meat. With a carpenter's hand saw he cut off two big pieces that weighed several pounds each. "Can you hobble on that foot?" he asked.

"Yes."

"Then stand outside the door and be quiet." Donovan walked toward the wolves carrying a chunk of meat in each hand. Both animals rose and stood waiting, tails waving. He began talking in a low, even voice, "I'm sorry I'm late. I'm glad you waited for me. I did get back with your suppers."

When he was about twenty or thirty feet away they began backing off. They never let him come closer. When he reached the spot where they'd been sitting he dropped the meat in the snow. "There you are," he said. "Good eating." He turned back to the cabin. As he retreated, the wolves came forward. They stopped at the meat and stood watching until he reached the cabin door. Only then did they pick up the meat and trot away, tails waving.

"Why, they're almost like dogs," I said. "Like pets. That's why you didn't kill them yesterday. You only shot to scare the black one away from me."

"You're getting smarter. He wouldn't have hurt you. He was curious. They're very inquisitive and amongst the smartest animals in the world. Real social, too. Care for one another a lot better than most humans. And they sure don't go around killing each other."

"Can you walk up to them? Can you pet them?"

"I don't try. I want them to stay wild. They come for this handout every day, which is tame enough. Maybe too tame. They shouldn't be putting much trust in men just because one is nice to them. But they're the only company I've had in two years." He walked around the cabin, got an armload of wood, and returned.

In a few minutes the cabin was warm again.

Donovan unloaded the sled and brought the canned food into the cabin and stacked it in a corner. The spare clothing he hung on pegs in the wall.

"Did — did anyone follow my trail?" I asked.

"There were no new tracks," he said. "Besides, it snowed again last night, so I don't expect much of your trail's left."

"What about the snowmobile?" I asked. "It's bright red and can be seen for a long distance."

"I heaped snow over it and packed it down. Nothing will show before spring thaw." He set to fixing supper.

No more was said until we'd eaten. Then I said, "I'll be able to leave in a few days."

14

"We'll talk about that later." he said. "You're rested now. I want to hear the whole story. What you told me yesterday sounded a little far fetched. You in trouble with the law?"

"No," I answered. "I flew up with a friend. We were taking supplies to a trapper. I told you that."

"People — especially kids — don't usually run around up here this far into winter without a good reason." He looked at me suspiciously. "Better spill your guts, kid."

It annoyed me that he was third degreeing me as if I were a criminal. "My reason's personal," I said. "It doesn't concern you."

"I'll be the judge of that. It appears there's more to this than just supplying a trapper. Start talking." And when I still hesitated, he added, "You're a guest in my home, such as it is. I want to know exactly what I'm dealing with. Could be I'll kick you out and let you shift for yourself. You say somebody killed your partner, but maybe it was you."

I thought of where I was — more than two thousand miles from home — in the empty, hostile Arctic — in the roughest kind of log cabin with a grouchy, unfriendly stranger and Ross dead. Suddenly my reason for being in the North didn't seem so important. I said uncertainly, "I don't know where to start."

"Try the beginning," he said dryly.

The beginning had been in another world, another time. It had been day before yesterday. "I guess a fight started it."

"You killed somebody and you've run away up here to hide out." It was a statement, not a question.

"It wasn't like that at all," I said defensively.

"All right, what was it like? It must have been mighty serious for you to chase up here this time of year. Shouldn't you be in school?"

I shook my head, searching for a way to tell him. "We've got these two debating clubs in school...."

"Debating clubs — in school! You telling me this is just a couple of kids getting into a slugfest over a debate?"

"The fight was just the beginning," I said.

"Holy smoke! Just a fight — a couple of kids. I should have guessed it'd be something like this the minute I saw you."

"We can forget it," I said stiffly. "You asked me."

"So I did. I asked for it. So let's have it."

I looked at the floor and rubbed my hands together. Finally I said, "I'm captain of one debating team. Scrapiron Davis, star tackle on the football team, is captain of the other.

"He's just average. This last debate I snowed him under. Afterward he laid for me and worked me over. It was the second time he'd done it."

"That's where you got the black eyes, swollen mouth, the face warped out of shape?"

"Yes. Except for this knot." I fingered the lump on my forehead. "I got it when I wrecked."

"Tough way to debate," he said dryly.

"Yes. Afterward my brother Rocky took me home and cleaned me up and I looked even worse. Dad would guess what had happened. He'd heard I hadn't put up much of a fight the first go around. He takes everything personally and he'd yelled and hollered at me for an hour then. He'd really be hot about it this time."

"What kind of fight did you put up?"

I thought about it. "Not so good, I guess. Scrapiron knocked me down about four times."

"What'd you do, just stand there and let him beat on you?"

"I tried to keep out of his way. He's pretty slow and sort of clumsy. It worked the first time. I thought I could do it again."

"He caught up with you and you got the full treatment?"

It didn't sound good, but I finally nodded, "I guess so."

"Kid," he asked quietly, "what would it take to make you fight?"

"I've never been in a fight," I confessed. "But it seems to me it ought to be something more important than just a school debate — something we did for fun."

"Can't say I blame your dad much. You should know how to defend yourself."

"Yes," I said, "I probably should." I thought about dad. College All-American, pro football three years. He's a partner in a

16

big law firm. I'd watched him in court and wondered if he really fought for his client or just to overwhelm the opposition.

"What about Rocky?" Donovan asked.

"My brother? He doesn't figure in this."

"I'll be the judge of that. I want to know a lot about you. You'll know why later. Now give. What about this brother?"

"Well, he takes after Dad, got a football scholarship. He and Dad have always stuck together. I'm not in their league, but while mother was alive I did all right. She kept Dad aware that I was on the swimming team, the track team and was captain of the debating team. After she died a few months ago Dad and Rocky seemed to get closer. I got farther away."

"But that wasn't why you chased up here in the dead of winter."

I shook my head. "I couldn't let dad see me with my face punched out of shape. He'd tower over me," I said thinking about it. "He'd beat me down with his size, his bull voice, his damning looks, condemning me with every breath for not making it a knock-down-drag-out fight. I'd had enough. I wanted to get away from him if even for a few hours. So I went to the hangar to talk to Ross. I've done it before. He understands how it is at home for me. I just don't belong. I know Ross because he flies my dad and his partners up here on fishing trips. I've been along before. Well, Ross was getting ready to fly supplies north. Everything for the trapper was loaded. Somebody called him to the phone and I sneaked into the plane and hid until we were too far to turn back. You know the rest."

"Let's say I know enough."

I could feel those brown eyes looking right into me. I knew what he was thinking. "I guess it sounds pretty silly to you," I said lamely. "It even does to me after all that's happened. But I just had to get away for a couple of days."

"Not silly," he said, "plain stupid. But I guess a man's allowed one stupid act in his life."

I looked at this unfriendly man and said, "Don't worry. I'll only be here a few days. This is the second. I figure about three more, then they'll begin looking for Ross. When he learns Ross is missing, Dad'll guess I'm with him after he contacts everybody I know and doesn't find me. He'll have planes out searching until I'm found. My dad will search everywhere."

"I doubt he's rich enough to do that. Everywhere is a mighty big place." He studied me those cold brown eyes, and went on. "Suppose they begin searching blind, over literally thousands of square miles. Even if you painted a billboard in the snow, the chances of it being seen are slim to none."

"What's that mean?" I asked. "Dad'll have a dozen planes out looking, maybe more."

"I've known of twenty planes looking for one missing person. They had the location pinpointed better than this and they never did find anyone. This is the biggest state in the union, it's rugged and still frontier, and on top of everything else, serious winter will be here any minute. First, they'll fly Ross's course. They may even find the burned plane. But they won't find hide nor hair of you. We don't even know where the cabin is from here, so we can't go there and wait. Besides, I don't much care for the idea of hanging around where I might get shot." He paused, staring hard at me. "Assuming that what you told me is true."

I shook my head. "It's all true." I thought of Dad: big, tough, confident. The kind of man who didn't know how to quit. "He'll find me," I said confidently. "He'll stay with it until he does. But you can call short wave and let someone know where I am."

"I don't have a short wave."

"Planes must bring you supplies and things like Ross was doing. How do you call them out?"

"In winter I don't. The tundra around here for miles is full of holes, rocks, frozen humps that don't show now because of the snow. A plane trying to land in winter would crack up sure. I have an agreement with a bush pilot to bring in supplies in the spring when the snow melts and then again in the fall. He lands on a gravel bar at the creek about a half mile away."

"We can hike out. I can make it. I'm in good shape. My father will pay you anything you ask."

Donovan shook his head. "It's two hundred miles to the nearest town. The country we'd have to cross is mighty rough.

18

Not mostly flat like around here. We could get caught in blizzards and have to sleep out. It'd take the better part of a month, maybe a whole month. I won't chance it in winter."

"There must be cabins along the way where we could rest a couple of days."

"I don't know where they are. Face it, kid, you're young and inexperienced. I could make those two hundred miles with a little luck. You can't, and if something happened to you I'd try to save you and we'd both die."

"I was a track man," I insisted stubbornly. "I swim a lot."

"It takes more than good shape and muscle. It takes a grown-up kind of courage."

"What do you mean by that?" I didn't like the insult.

"Not sure I can explain it. I know it when I see it. It comes from in here." He tapped his chest. "Sometimes it takes years to develop. Some never get it. It makes you face up to problems, sort of roll up your sleeves and wade in."

"What if you lose?"

"Losing's no disgrace. Quitting is."

Ross had said almost the same thing back in Seattle. It hadn't made me angry then, but coming from this big man it did. "You saying I'm a quitter?"

"You quit on that Scrapiron guy. You ran away from your old man."

"I didn't quit. I got out of a situation I couldn't handle the best way I could."

"Call it what you like. I say you quit," Donovan said flatly. "And that's what I'm afraid you'd do with me on a two hundred mile hike out. I know this land. I know these northern blizzards and they're murder. I know what it takes to survive. You're still a boy. Something's going to have to happen to you to take out the boy and put a lot of man in you."

I had no answer to that. I said, "I can't stay here. Rocky and Dad'll think I'm dead. I've got to get back," I insisted. "I've just got to."

"Look," his voice was tough, emotionless. "You don't like it here. I don't want you here. If I'd wanted a partner I wouldn't have picked a kid still wet behind the ears. But you are here and there's nothing either of us can do about it."

"What about Ross?" I challenged. "There's a murderer out here somewhere who could come after us now."

"There's probably more than one murder out here keeping clear of the law. That doesn't mean he'll go wandering around in the weather looking for you." The way he said it, I felt sure he knew more than he was saying. A twinge of fear crawled up my spine.

"I have to do something," I said.

"What?"

"Dad'll have planes out searching those thousands of miles. A dozen planes can cover a lot of country. That cuts the odds on finding me down a lot, doesn't it?"

"If he has enough planes out."

"He will," I said confidently. "One of them could spot this cabin. It's in the open. Why — why tomorrow I'll wait outside. If they fly over I'll wave my red sweater. They'll see it and send a chopper out to pick me up. Well, couldn't they?"

Donovan shrugged his shoulders. "I can see I'm not going to convince you otherwise, so try to think it out. This is the end of the second day since you left. You said the pilot planned to return to Seattle immediately. Maybe your dad guesses you're with Ross and begins to worry today. It'll be tomorrow before he can do much. Give the pilots a day to fly your route and find Ross and the plane. Since there's no sign of you, they might figure you didn't fly north with Ross. But, assuming your dad's sure, it'll take a couple more days to begin an all-out search. That gives you about another four days here before you can expect anything."

"I guess so," I said. Put that way it sounded pretty bleak, but I couldn't give up without at least trying. "I'll start watching tomorrow. Some plane could come over sooner, couldn't it?"

"It's possible, but don't count on it. Planes seldom fly over here in winter. And if the weather turns bad, no amount of money is going to buy a search."

"I don't want to miss any chance," I said.

Donovan looked at me and shook his head. "Have it your way, kid."

- 3 -

I wanted to talk more. There were questions I wanted to ask, but Donovan was through. He filled the stove with wood, closed the draft, and blew out the light. He flopped on his bunk without a word.

I crawled into my sleeping bag and lay staring up at the dark ceiling, thinking of this cabin somewhere in the wilds of Alaska and this strange, unfriendly man. Even if he had rescued me, I was glad I'd have to put up with him only a few days.

But Donovan was an odd one. He didn't fit the description of the rough, dirty, bewhiskered trapper I'd always seen pictures of. This man sounded educated. There was a shelf of books above his bunk. He was smooth-shaven, but his hair was long. His clothes were rough, they had to be for this climate. But they were neat. He reminded me a little of one of Dad's law partners. He had an air that seemed to say he could walk into any business office, building, or house and feel comfortable. Yet he was living the roughest kind of life and he called this cabin home. Strange.

I thought of this country: huge, bleak, desolate, locked in Arctic cold. My ears were tuned for any strange sounds that might be alive in this frigid world. I heard the whisper of wind at the cabin's corners. A swaying branch tapped the log wall. There was a sudden snapping and cracking, then silence. Some big animal, a moose probably, smashing his way through the brush. Then there was silence again — silence broken by a sound so soft I wasn't sure at first I was hearing it. It seemed a part of the wind, the night, this ice-locked land. It rose to a clear, sad note of long-

21

ing that swelled in volume until it filled the night and hung quivering on the glacial silence. I had never heard a lone wolf's voice, but I knew it instantly. It died away so softly I was not sure just when it ended. It rose again soaring to a high, clear call. Then it faded into the massive stillness. For a moment the earth was utterly mute, waiting.

Then, far off, in a different direction, came a soft, bell-clear answer. The first voice called again and was answered. Then they rose together and faded away. It was the voice of the wild and primitive, of this mysterious, forbidding land.

From his bunk Donovan said, "Hear that, kid?"

"Yes," I said.

"Wolf calling for a mate and found one. Concert in the Arctic. Love at forty below." He sounded pleased.

The wolf duet finally ended. Again I heard the soft whisper of the wind, the branch scratching against the log, and Donovan's even breathing. The stove went out. Freezing night air crept through the chinked logs. The interior temperature began to drop.

I thought of my home high in the hills above Seattle. My room was bigger than this whole cabin. I could lie in bed and look down on the city, the spider-web pattern of streets and highways, the bug-like traffic. Beyond, the ink-black harbor where the lighted ferries and the black bulk of ships crept in and out. I thought of Dad and Rocky. Rocky was probably out with some girlfriend. Dad, if he was worried yet, could be on the phone checking everyone who knew me. I wondered what he'd think if he knew where I was and the man I was with. And again I wondered about Donovan. What kind of man was he? What was he doing out here alone, a seemingly educated man? Thinking of him I finally slept.

Next morning after breakfast I put on my parka and sat in front of the cabin holding my sweater ready to wave. I stared at the empty sky. As soon as my ankle felt better — maybe tomorrow — I'd build a signal fire.

Donovan came from the cabin carrying a rifle. He watched me for several minutes and said nothing. He started to leave, then said, "The wolves may come around but they won't bother you.

They'll just sit and look. I left a chunk of meat on the table. Feed them if you like. Do just as I did." Then he slogged off through the brush and disappeared.

Finally my eyes started hurting from staring so hard and from the glare of light off the snow. I closed them to let them rest and concentrated instead on listening for the sound of a plane. When I opened my eyes again, I became aware of the wolves. I had no idea how long they'd been sitting there watching me. The small grey one that Donovan called Fawn cocked her sharp head first one way, then the other. Blackie dropped his big head and gave me that disconcerting, measured stare.

I froze. Wild stories of wolves attacking people raced through my head. But they just sat and watched, and gradually my near panic subsided. Finally I rose carefully, gripping the axe in both hands, and began edging toward the cabin. The wolves watched.

I went inside, closed the door and sat on the bench. My mouth was dry and my heart hammered. Finally my heart settled back to normal and I peeked out the door. The wolves still sat like a pair of waiting dogs.

The slab of moose meat lay on the table. I thought of Donovan's words, "They won't bother you. Feed them if you like." I peeked out again. They waited expectantly. Why not, I thought. I can take the axe with me. I dreaded the thought of facing them, but something kept pushing me. I cut two big chunks of meat. Then, carrying the axe in my right hand, I opened the door, left it open, and began walking slowly toward them. They both rose. Again Blackie dropped that big head and studied me. Fawn tilted her head both ways and wagged her tail. I had to swallow a couple of times before my voice would come.

"I've brought you something," I said. "You ready to eat? You've sure got it soft. Choice moose steaks every day. You know what these would cost where I come from?"

I figured I'd gone as close as I dared and was about to stop when they began backing away. They continued to back off as I approached. I advanced to the spot where they'd sat, dropped the meat, and moved slowly toward the cabin. "There you are," I said, "Dinner is served." They advanced to the meat, stopped, and watched to make sure I wasn't coming toward them. Then they picked up the steaks and trotted away, heads and tails high.

I went inside and closed the cabin door. I felt an elation and satisfaction I'd never known in my life before.

I didn't see the wolves again that day. I watched the ice-blue sky the remainder of the daylight hours and tried to visualize what it would be like when a plane came. It would explode over those distant white mountains, and flying low, would streak across the flat tundra straight for me. The pilot would see me wave, wheel the plane around for a confirming look, and I'd soon be on my way home.

Donovan returned as the day was dropping behind the white mountains. He had two muskrats, a fox, and another animal I later learned was an ermine. "No plane." It was not a question.

"I didn't really expect one so soon. I just want to be ready."

He nodded and went inside. I followed. He noticed the meat was gone. "Any trouble with the wolves?"

"No," I said.

He looked at me. My eyes were sore and puffy. I was rubbing them, "You're going to ruin your eyes out there if you keep up your vigil." He went to a metal chest in the corner and rummaged through it. A few minutes later he handed me a pair of strange glasses with narrow horizontal slits instead of lenses. "The natives use these to prevent snow blindness," he said.

After supper Donovan skinned out the animals and stretched the hides on small frames. I melted snow, washed the dishes, and it was time to turn in.

The next morning I tested my ankle and decided I could get around well enough to build my signal fire. After breakfast, I pulled on my mukluks and parka, took the hand axe, and opened the door. A soft, fine snow was falling. The visibility was poor. No planes would fly over today. As helpless and lonely as I felt, I still limped around for an hour gathering dry brush and limbs into a pile. Then I went inside and sat. My head overflowed with thoughts of home. Finally I went to Donovan's bookshelf hoping for something to take my mind off my problems.

There wasn't much that interested me. It was a pretty small collection: a one volume encyclopedia, a book on trapping, another on weather, a dictionary, a history of mythology, and several pamphlets on wilderness foods and survival that I thought I'd look at if no one rescued me in the next few days. There were several paperback novels, and collections of mysteries. I pulled a heavy hardcover book down for a closer look. It was a selection of novels and stories by Jack London. I figured I find something interesting in it, since I enjoyed "To Build a Fire" when we read it in school.

I stoked the stove and tried to get comfortable, but I couldn't concentrate on reading. My mind kept going back to what had happened to Ross and to the thought of rescue. I couldn't sit more than a few minutes without jumping up to see if the weather had cleared.

Nothing changed during the next few days. As if to taunt me, the nights turned clear and cold, the sky so full of stars I couldn't believe it was the same one over Seattle. During the day, the snow sifted steadily down. It wasn't heavy, but it was never clear enough for rescue planes. My situation grew more hopeless with each hour. The days would have been deadly monotonous but for the books and the wolves. Each morning Donovan donned his parka, took up the rifle and left, usually without a word. He seldom brought back fur. Possibly, I thought, he wanted to be alone. He was a morose, quiet man. I had the feeling he was unhappy. Once I brought it up. We had finished supper and I said, "Is this a bad year for trapping?"

"Not that I know of."

"I don't see many skins," I went on. "There's a few on that line in the shed. Have you more somewhere else?"

"What you see is it."

Then I blurted out what had been bothering me for days. "You don't work at it very hard."

"I'm out almost every day."

"You seldom bring anything back. Trappers trap to get animals, to make money, don't they? You don't seem to try."

"I get all I need." Then he added, "You're pretty sharp for a city kid. What're you driving at?"

My confidence was shaky, but I'd started it and my curiosity carried me on. "You don't look like pictures of trappers I've seen. I don't think you talk like one either."

"And so....?"

"I don't think you are one." I could almost see the toughness come up in that craggy face. His brown eyes turned darker and narrowed, his chin was set. Roughness was in his voice when he spoke.

"What I am, why I'm here, what I do, and where I came from is no concern of yours."

"I was just curious."

"Don't be." Donovan rose and walked out of the cabin.

Every day I waited for the snow to stop and the sky to clear. I finished the Jack London book. And I fed the wolves. I no longer took the axe along for protection. They always backed off. Fawn was more inclined to trust me than Blackie. He still kept that thirty or so feet between us and he always dropped his head to stare straight at me. But now I knew that was just his habit. I could get within twenty feet of Fawn and talk to her as if she were a person. I enjoyed the way she cocked her head, lifted her lips in a wolfish smile, and ran out her pink tongue as she listened. Sometimes I felt as if she understood. I'd never had a pet and being this close to a wild wolf was strange and exciting.

I wondered if Dad had ever seen a wild wolf and what he'd think if he could see me now talking and playing with her. I had fed them one day and was talking a bunch of nonsense to them when I looked up and Donovan stood there watching me. He had come up as quietly as the wolves. I felt embarrassed and said, "I guess it sounds silly talking to an animal this way."

"Not at all," he said. "For two years they've been my only friends, my only company. I talk to them every day. I think they understand and they never argue back."

26

I looked up expecting to see the first smile on that craggy face. It was not there.

I was surprised how fast I was adjusting to this northern land. I waited now and listened for the night sounds to break the Arctic silence. I learned to distinguish between the hunting cry of a wolf pack and their nightly singing that filled the land. All these sounds blended together and told me all was well out there in the wild and I, in my sleeping bag on the bunk, was a part of it.

It made me think of the book I'd been reading the past couple of days, the *Collected Poems of Robert Service*. It was a well thumbed volume, and I could see why Donovan had it with him. The author had roamed around the North and his poems were as much stories and songs of the people, the animals, and the great wild Arctic as they were verses. Some, like "The Shooting of Dan McGrew" and "The Cremation of Sam McGee," were humorous. Others, like "The Spell of the Yukon" and "The Land God Forgot," were serious, even sad. Listening to the sounds of the night, I recalled a few lines of one I'd read that day, "The Ballad of the Northern Lights."

> So we came at last to a tundra vast and
>   dark and grim and lone;
> And there was the little lone moose trail,
>   and we knew it for our own.

The tenth day the snow stopped. I had fed the wolves, watched them leave, and was standing inside the door looking off at the distant mountains when a patch of blue sky appeared. Hope surged alive in me. Maybe my dad would still have planes searching, just waiting for a chance. They would take advantage of the break in the weather to scour the country for me.

I raced to build up my pile of wood, certain that at any moment I'd hear the sound of a plane. I knew no one might come now, but I had to try. The new snow made my task more difficult. The wolves sat a little way off and watched my every move. By the time I had a pile big enough, I was sweating inside my parka.

I went into the cabin to put on a dry shirt and eat something. When I came back out to begin my vigil, the sky had closed in and the fine snow had started again. I stared into the grayness until my eyes ached and my neck was stiff. Finally I knew that Donovan was right. No one was coming to my rescue. There was just me standing alone in this immense and empty land, beneath the cloudy sky.

I sat down in the snow and put my head in my hands. I wanted to cry but I was too old and too big. The silence of this frigid, inhospitable land was a weight beating me down. I had never felt so alone, so lost, so helpless.

The penetrating cold finally brought me to my senses. When I looked up, there, not fifty yards off, two men came across the tundra toward me. Both carried rifles. I felt an urge to run, to hide, or grab the gun leaning just inside the cabin door. Then I thought this might mean my rescue.

I rose and waited. One was tall and thick chested. The other was short and stocky. They stopped on the other side of my brush pile. The hoods of their parkas were thrown back and long, scraggly hair hung to their shoulders. The tall one's hair was jet black and matched his eyes. He looked at me as Blackie, the wolf, had that first morning. His eyes bored into me and suddenly I was even more uncomfortable and wary. The short one's hair would have been some shade of blond if it had been clean. His face was flat, round, and of no particular expression. His eyes were a washed-out blue, as empty as the sky.

The big one glanced over my head at the smoke coming from the stovepipe and said, "Thought Donovan was home. Didn't expect to find a kid here."

"Sure didn't," the blond one shook his head.

"I've only been here ten days," I said.

They both nodded. The big one asked, "You gonna be livin' here now?"

"No. I'm Joel Rogers, but people call me Joe. I crashed in a snowmobile a couple of miles from here a few days ago. Mr. Donovan found me and brought me to his cabin." I thought better of telling them about Ross and the airplane. At least for now.

"Haven't seen th' wreck," the big one said. "Must be covered with snow?"

"Yes. You fellows trappers?"

The black eyes never left my face, "You could say that — in a way. I'm Hank," he jerked his head toward the smaller one, "he's Emmitt. What's the brush pile for?"

"To signal a rescue plane," I answered.

"Didn't see no plane."

Emmitt nodded, "Didn't see one." His voice was high and whiny.

"A plane'll come." I didn't feel very convincing when I said it.

"Not many planes fly over here in winter," Hank said.

"That's for sure," Emmitt said. "Not many."

"My father will keep looking for me."

"Pretty expensive," Hank said.

"Plenty expensive," Emmitt echoed.

"He won't give up."

"Must have a full sock," Hank observed.

I didn't answer.

Finally Hank asked, "How long you figure they been lookin'?"

"About five days. Maybe six."

"If they don't find you by now, they'll call off the search. 'Specially in this weather."

"That's for sure," Emmitt nodded.

I was getting annoyed at Emmitt parroting Hank, but I said, "Then I'll find another way. I've got to get back."

Hank said, "How about hikin' out?"

"I asked Donovan, but he won't take me. He says it's too dangerous, I couldn't make it."

Those black eyes measured me and again I had that uncomfortable, wary feeling. "You could make it," he said in a flat voice.

"Sure you could," Emmitt agreed. "Anybody can see that."

Mike Donovan stepped out of the brush a hundred feet away. His rifle was cradled in his arm.

Hank and Emmitt immediately turned quiet. I could feel the tension grow as Donovan approached.

Donovan stopped close and when he spoke his voice was cold, "You fellows are pretty far off your range."

"Saw the smoky fire. Thought you might be burnin' out," Hank said.

"Yeah, we come to see," Emmitt said.

"No such luck." Donovan's smile was tight and thin. I could almost see the sparks jumping between these three.

"Maybe another time," Hank said.

"Another time," Emmitt echoed.

Hank's eyes met Emmitt's. They began walking away. Hank said over his shoulder, "Seen some pretty big wolf tracks around."

"They're friends of mine."

"Mighty odd friends."

Donovan and I watched them disappear into the brush. I said, "You don't like them."

Donovan shook his head. "Do you?"

"No. There's something about Hank, the way he looks at me like — like he'd just as soon shoot me as not."

"I've felt the same thing. Emmitt is just a mocking bird. He can't even think unless Hank tells him to. But that Hank is a deadly dangerous man."

"Hank said they were trappers, sort of. What's that mean?"

"I've been trying to figure that out for almost two years. They showed up suddenly and began living in a fairly new cabin somebody built, maybe just for them. It's about four or five miles from here — a lot closer than I want 'em. I asked the bush pilot who brings in my supplies about them. All he could learn was that another pilot had flown them out and settled them in and later visited them two or three times. Hank and Emmitt never go out to any of the towns, and the pilot who brought them out here said he hadn't seen them in almost a year."

"Maybe he knows why they're out here."

"He's disappeared. Nobody knows what happened to him. I have learned a few things about Hank and Emmitt," Donovan continued. "They're not trappers. They've got a small line but they don't seem to work it. They were strangers to the country and how to live here. Only this winter have they come up with proper clothing. And until this season their rifles were small, not big, hard-hitting guns, the kind you need in this country."

"Then what're they doing here?"

"That's the big question. The only things you can do in the bush are trap, prospect, and hunt. They do none of them."

"They sound kind of mysterious," I said.

Donovan nodded slowly. "One thing they could be doing and they wouldn't be the first. They could be hiding from the law. And that could take in hundreds of reasons." He shrugged finally and said, "I suppose you'll keep waiting to light a signal fire?"

"Yes," and when he added nothing to that I said, "A plane could still come, couldn't it?"

"Sure. But the chances are getting slimmer every day." With that he went into the cabin.

I watched him go. A strange, lonely man with no warmth, no sympathy or love for anything but a couple of wild wolves. Why was he up here living in frigid, primitive isolation? Was he, too, running from the law? He might be right to be suspicious of Hank and Emmitt, but I could see little difference between them and Mike Donovan.

I thought of spending the rest of the winter cooped up in a tiny cabin in this wilderness with such a man for company and those other two for neighbors. No way! I was going to get away from here no matter what I had to do, what chances I had to take.

- 4 -

The sun was out and I had a larger fire pile built by noon the next day. As usual Donovan had taken off across the tundra several hours before. I had just finished when the wolves arrived. Again they had come in utter silence. One moment there was nothing. The next they were sitting side by side watching me expectantly. I'd got over the small pulse of fear that raced up my spine each time I was surprised by them.

I got two chunks of meat, fed them and talked to them several minutes, then watched as they trotted off through the brush with their prizes. Once again I settled down to studying the sky. Not a hawk, eagle, owl, or ptarmigan crossed that frigid blue bowl.

For five more days the weather was clear and my monotonous sky watch continued. Donovan disappeared almost every morning. He'd return about dusk, seldom with more than one or two animals to skin out. He said nothing of where he went or what he did. He became more of a mystery every day.

During this time I explored close to the cabin, never straying more than a few seconds dash from the fire pile in case a plane appeared. Except for the books, the daily visits of the wolves were the only break in this routine.

Each day I fed them and finally began experimenting with a different approach. I no longer fed them as soon as they arrived. I let them sit and watch me while I talked to them. I'd never had any experience with animals. In the city there was a leash law and the few dogs never ran free. I was intrigued and fascinated by this close association with a pair of wild Alaskan wolves.

I enjoyed talking to them though the conversation was a bit one-sided. To Blackie I'd say, "You're not half as fierce as you look. You don't fool me. You're a lucky slob. You've got the prettiest mate in the whole territory — you know that? I just hope you're smart enough to appreciate her. Oh, you know it, huh. Then why don't you show it instead of sitting there glowering at me like some back street tough?"

And to Fawn I'd say, "How come you hang out with this guy? He's no glamour wolf. With your looks you could have any wolf on the tundra. Oh, so you think he's good looking. Well, there's no accounting for taste." They'd tip their heads first one way then the other, their ears jumping back and forth as they listened and seemed to try to understand.

I no longer gave them their meat in two big slabs. I kept them there by trying to coax them closer. I cut the meat into chunks and tossed the pieces to first one, then the other. Each time I tossed the meat a bit short so they had to come forward to get it. I got Blackie within about thirty feet, but that was his limit. He simply stood there, head down, ready to retreat.

Fawn came so close I could see the individual hairs on her face, the dark pupils of her eyes. From that close distance I fed and talked to her. Finally I got her to utter a low breathy bark when I held out the meat and said, "You want it, say so."

With each passing day my confidence that a plane would come eroded further. By the end of what I figured would be the tenth day of searching I kept the vigil only because I had nothing else to do.

The next afternoon, after the wolves had eaten and gone, I was staring at the empty sky when Hank and Emmitt came. They looked as dirty and scraggly-haired as before. Again those black, emotionless eyes of Hank's gave me that wary, uncomfortable feeling.

"Plane didn't come," was his greeting. It wasn't a question.
"No."

"Been a long time now. Ten, eleven days since they started lookin'."

"Eleven today," I said. I felt Hank had been keeping track.

"Won't come then."

"Nope, won't come." I couldn't tell if Emmitt's colorless eyes were looking at me or just staring in my direction.

"How'd you get here anyway?" Hank asked.

I didn't answer. I was sure they hadn't just happened by.

Hank said, "Me and Emmitt been thinkin'. Donovan won't hike you out, you say?"

"That's right."

"You wanta go bad?"

"Yes," I said, "I've got to."

Hank scuffed his feet in the snow. Then his head came up and those black eyes hit me like a physical force. "Me and Emmitt just might walk you out."

"All the way?"

"Wouldn't have to. We know a man sixty, seventy miles from here who's got short wave. We walk you to his place. He can call out a plane. He has for us. Plane on skis can land at his place. But it'll cost. You sure your old man'll pay?"

"Anything you ask."

"What's he do that he's got so much cash?"

"He's a lawyer. A trial lawyer. He tries a lot of big criminal cases."

"Criminal lawyer, huh."

Emmitt said, "Maybe we better think about this some more."

"Shut up." Hank kept frowning at his feet.

I could feel him hesitating and suddenly I couldn't bear to miss this one chance to get out of this ice box, to get away from Donovan, to return home. I disregarded my doubts about these two, my dislike of Emmitt, my fear of Hank, and Donovan's warning that he was a dangerous man, and said quickly, "If you've got any problems with the law my dad'll fight your case and not charge you a dime. He'll also pay whatever you ask to take me out."

"What makes you think we've got law troubles?" Hank asked.

"Yeah, what makes you think?" Emmitt parroted.

I knew then they did have troubles, but I said, "Nothing. Not a thing. I just tossed that in as an added inducement."

"Money's the only inducement we need," Hank said.

"Yeah, money." Emmitt rubbed his fingers together in a well-known money gesture.

"Takin' you out could be expensive," Hank pointed out. "It'll be takin' our time and know-how. Also, we got Donovan to consider. We ain't exactly friendly." Those black eyes drilled into me, measuring me, gauging me. "Could cost as much as three, four thousand — maybe more."

"How will my father get the money to you?"

"I haven't said we'd do it yet."

"I thought that's what you were leading up to. Why you came over?"

"You're a pretty smart kid."

"No," I said hastily. "I just want to get out of here — fast."

Hank's eyes pinned me like a bug to a wall. "All right. We'll take you. Before you fly out with the bush pilot I'll give you a name. Your old man sends the money to him. Cash, no checks. He'll see we get it. Your old man better come through or some friends of ours will pay him a visit."

"That's for sure," Emmitt said.

"You'll get your money."

"All right. It's up to you to shake Donovan."

"He leaves almost every morning. I don't know where he goes."

"We've been keepin' tabs on him. He just rams around the country," Hank said.

"Just rams around," Emmitt said.

"Soon as he gets out of sight I'll take off," I said. "Which direction is your place?"

Hank pointed, "Off there about five miles. Follow our trail when we leave and I'll blaze a few trees so you know you're on the right track. You won't see the cabin until you're right on it. It's pretty well hidden in the brush. Another thing, if Donovan spots our tracks and says anything, you'd better be ready with some kind of story about us just passin' by."

"I will." I was getting excited about leaving. "I don't know how soon I can take off. He goes different directions each day. I'll have to be careful he's not going toward your place or I could run into him. Some days he doesn't leave until noon or later. It could be two or three days before it's safe."

"We'll hang around the cabin and wait. Bring a sleepin' bag and grub for three day's tough hikin'. Canned beans, sandwiches, things like that. Get to our place as fast as you can. With luck we should have a six or seven hour head start.

"Donovan won't begin lookin' for you right off. He'll figure you're out rammin' around like he does. When he does get suspicious and begins to look, it oughta be dark. With no full moon he'll have trouble separatin' out tracks. It'll take a little time to figure out what you're up to. Then he'll light out for our place. With luck we'll have a good start. When we get to where we're goin' we call out a plane. You should be back in civilization before Donovan gets near."

"You won't have any trouble with him over this?"

"We're headed for trouble some time. I can feel it."

"Yeah," Emmitt said darkly. "Plenty of trouble."

"But not over this," Hank said. "By the time he gets to where you take off we'll be long gone. He'll know. He's no fool. But he won't be able to prove a thing. Leave as soon as you can and make tracks to our place. We'll be packed and ready."

"Shall I bring a rifle?"

"It'll just be added weight. We'll have guns."

"Yeah, we'll have 'em," Emmitt said.

A couple of minutes later they disappeared back into the brush.

Donovan returned about dusk. He had a pair of ptarmigans, a rabbit, fox, and another white weasel. We had the ptarmigan for supper. Afterward Donovan said, "Didn't I see Hank and Emmitt's tracks?"

"Yes. I was at the fire pile. Hank said, 'So the plane didn't come. Didn't figure it would.' Then they left."

Donovan nodded, "Hank's right about the plane. You plan on sitting outside waiting some more?"

"I don't mind it," I said. "I'll try a few more days."

"Sure." Donovan went to skinning the fox.

I went to bed early. I was so nervous I was afraid Donovan's sharp eyes would spot something wrong and he'd become suspicious. After Donovan had blown out the lamp and turned in, I lay awake thinking and planning what I'd take. Tonight, I told myself, could be the last I'd spend in this cabin with this man. In three or four days I'd be home with Rocky and Father — my own people. This nightmare would be over.

Next morning Donovan was in no rush to leave. He tinkered about the cabin, cleaned his rifle and oiled it. He mended a rip in his parka, cleaned the ashes from the stove, shook out his bedding, and carefully made the bed.

I stood it as long as I could, then casually asked, "You going out today?"

"Think I'll take the day off."

So it went. I fed the wolves, talked to Fawn, and once again watched the empty sky. Donovan was interested in the way I fed the wolves. "You could have Fawn eating out of your hand soon. But not Blackie."

"No," I said. "Not Blackie."

Night swept down off the distant mountains like an incoming tide. We ate supper and I crawled into my sleeping bag.

Donovan left right after breakfast. He slipped into his parka, picked up the rifle, and walked out without a look or word. He headed in exactly the direction I'd have to go to reach Hank and Emmitt's.

Another wasted day.

Doubts crowded in upon me. Maybe Hank and Emmitt would tire of waiting and refuse to take me. Or they might come over to see what was holding me up. Donovan might see them and he'd immediately become suspicious. Maybe they'd decided facing Donovan was too big a risk. My doubts drove me to the edge of panic and I had to say sternly to myself, "Cut it out. Quit imagining problems. It's going to be all right. They know you may have trouble getting away. You've got to be patient. Wait. Wait."

Donovan returned with a single rabbit that he skinned and we had for supper. I went to bed early.

Next morning I watched Donovan prepare to leave. He took a long time getting into his parka, checking the rifle, making sure he had extra shells. Finally he left. He stood in front of the cabin for several minutes as if trying to decide which way to go. I had the suddenly horrible feeling he knew I was waiting for him to leave and was deliberately baiting me. Finally he took off — going in the opposite direction I'd have to go.

I should have waited at least a half hour to be sure he was gone. But I was too keyed up. I grabbed my sleeping bag, stuffed cans of food into my pack, and slung it over my shoulders.

I slipped into the nearby brush and ran until my heart felt like it was tearing my chest apart. I found several trees Hank had blazed. I was headed right and didn't look for more markings.

The sleeping bag and pack were heavy, the snow deep, the walking rough. But I didn't mind. I was on my way. I was going home at last.

I was lucky it hadn't snowed again. Hank and Emmitt's tracks made it a little easier. I set a fast pace, but was finally forced to stop to rest. Slow down, I warned myself, don't wear yourself out before you get to Hank and Emmitt's. From their cabin it would be another sixty or so miles. I started off again before I was completely rested.

A little more than an hour later I came suddenly on their cabin snugly hidden in the brush. When I walked in they were rolling sleeping bags and getting into their parkas. Ten minutes later we were on our way.

I thought I was in good shape and for school activities I was. But this demanded much more. I breathed a lot of frigid air and my lungs finally began to hurt. Emmitt showed me how to expel my breath against the side of the parka hood, then when I breathed in I got part of the warm air. It helped. But they had to stop often to give me a break. On one I opened a can of beans, whittled a stick for a spoon and gobbled them down.

Once again we resumed the same fast pace.

Hank and Emmitt chewed jerky. They gave me a piece and I chewed as we hiked. There was no talking. That breath was needed for walking.

The last of daylight caught us as we left the flat tundra and trudged up into the foothills. Darkness brought added cold. But Hank didn't stop. We hiked at least another hour then entered a small grove of trees. In the center was a log cabin.

The cabin was ice cold and musty. But there was a lamp with oil and the stove was laid with wood ready to light.

Soon the fire was crackling merrily and the place began to warm up. I opened a couple of more cans of beans and ate them cold. Then I spread my sleeping bag on the floor and wearily crawled in. I asked Hank how far it was to this friend with the short wave and he said casually, "Bout forty, fifty miles."

"Can we keep ahead of Donovan?"

"If you can keep up."

"I'll make it." Then I asked, "What's this friend's name?"

"Don't remember. You know, Emmitt?"

"No."

"Don't matter anyway," Hank said. "Names don't mean much up here." From under his parka he brought out a pistol and began wiping the moisture off it.

"I didn't know you brought that along," Emmitt said.

"I've carried it since I was fifteen, you know that. I'd feel naked without it." He unloaded the pistol and aimed it at various spots in the room. Hank had changed the past hours. There was a kind of impersonal toughness about him I hadn't felt before. I remembered Donovan's words, "That Hank is a dangerous man." Suddenly I wished I hadn't come, but there was nothing I could do about it now.

- 5 -

A blast of Arctic air shook me awake. It took a few seconds to come fully alert and locate the direction of the air. I turned my head and a rush of fear brought me bolt upright. The door was wide open and silhouetted against the night was the giant bulk of a man holding a rifle. Then the figure spoke and I recognized the voice of Mike Donovan. "Kid, light the lamp."

It took a minute to scramble up, fumble for a match in the dark, and light the wick. The moment light flooded the room Hank and Emmitt started up from their sleeping bags rubbing their eyes. "What's goin' on?" Hank demanded sleepily.

"Yeah, what?" Emmitt echoed.

Donovan kicked the door closed but kept the rifle pointed at the two men. He said to me, "Get your sleeping bag. We're leaving."

"I'm not going," I said. "These fellows are taking me out where I can catch a plane. I'm going home." Then a thought struck me. "How'd you get here so fast?"

"I made a swing out across the tundra and ran across some mighty fresh tracks. They weren't mine. Who else would three sets of fresh tracks belong to? I put two and two together. Hank and Emmitt visited you six days ago. You couldn't make a deal with me to walk you out so you made one with them. Then you waited for a time you figured I'd be gone all day and took off. What'd they say they'd do for you?"

Hank reached stealthily for his rifle leaning against the wall. Donovan's rifle immediately centered on him. "Don't try it." His voice was icy.

Hank hesitated, his outstretched hand still reaching. There was a dry click as Donovan pulled back the hammer. "I won't say it again."

I looked into Donovan's craggy face and set jaw and my mouth went dry. Donovan would kill Hank.

Hank knew it too. His hand dropped. He sat back on the floor, but his black eyes were like a cat's waiting to pounce. "Your hand," his voice was calm. "Play it."

Emmitt was edging toward his own rifle and Donovan swung and covered him. "Relax, Emmitt," he said. "This is not your night to howl."

Emmitt relaxed.

Donovan picked up Emmitt's rifle and added it to the other against the wall. Then he said to me again, "What'd they tell you, kid?"

"They'd take me out."

"All the way?"

"We'd only have to walk fifty or sixty miles. They'd take me to another trapper who's got short wave. He'd call for a plane to fly me out."

"What'll it cost?"

"Three or four thousand. Hank would give me a name before I left. The money was to be delivered to that man in cash."

"And you went for it."

"I want to go home."

"You'll never make it this way. Come on, we're leaving."

Hank was on his feet, fists clenched. "Who do you think you are bustin' in here throwin' your weight around? We made a deal with th' kid and he went for it. We're takin' him out. So you back off. Don't buy more trouble than you can handle."

"No trouble." Donovan's rifle still centered on Hank's middle, but he spoke to me, "Unload those rifles. You know how?"

I'd watched Donovan unload his rifle every day. I picked up each and ejected the shells. Donovan held out his hand and I gave them to him. Then he said to Hank and Emmitt, "Turn out your pockets. I want all the shells on the table."

Each produced about a dozen shells. Donovan pocketed them. "Now get your sleeping bag. We're leaving."

I'd gotten over the shock of seeing Donovan and now anger smothered my fear of the big man. Here was my one chance to leave this ice-locked country and he was ruining it. "You get out," I shot at him. "I'm going with Hank and Emmitt. I want out of this country and away from you. You're not stopping me."

"Pick up that sleeping bag and your pack," his voice was deadly quiet, "or I'll drag you out by the hair without them."

For a moment our eyes clashed, then I bent, rolled up the sleeping bag and roped it to the pack.

Hank stood there, fists clenched, a big cat poised to spring. His black eyes were shooting raw hate at Donovan. He was held back only by the pointing rifle. Hank, I was sure, could give Donovan all the fight he wanted and more.

I straightened to swing the pack on my back — and kept swinging it with all my strength into Donovan's surprised face. Startled, Donovan jerked aside to avoid the bag and threw up an arm to push it away. The rifle muzzle dropped. The rest happened in a split second. Hank launched himself at Donovan, big hands reaching. But Donovan was surprisingly fast. He slapped the sleeping bag aside, side-stepped Hank's rush and brought the rifle barrel down on his head with a sickening crack. Hank collapsed on hands and knees. A track of blood coursed down the side of his face.

Donovan said in the softest voice, "Pick up the sleeping bag, kid, and no more cute tricks."

Hank got dizzily to his feet holding his head. He swayed, glaring at Donovan, his voice deadly, "No man does that to me and lives."

Donovan said, "Don't throw empty threats at me."

"If you knew who I was down south, you'd know they're not empty threats."

"I don't know who you were, I know what you are up here. That's good enough."

"Then you know I don't bluff."

"Come off it. All three of us are up here for the same reason. Nobody on earth cares a damn what we do to each other. If we chew each other up into mincemeat we'll save the authorities in the south forty-eight the trouble of doing it. That makes any threat pretty empty."

"Not to me." Hank wiped blood from the side of his face. His burning black eyes never left Donovan. He pointed a trembling finger, "Remember, every time you step outside or turn around, me and Emmitt will be somewhere, watchin'. Maybe we'll be ahead of you. Maybe behind. But we'll be there waitin' for th' right time, th' right place. We've got nothin' but time. Mister, you're a dead man. Count on it."

"Aren't you forgetting that up here you don't have a gang to hide behind, to protect you?"

"Don't need one. I know a hundred ways to take you."

"That I believe," Donovan said dryly. "You've had two years. Why haven't you done it?"

"Didn't have a reason. Now I do."

Donovan's smile was wintry. "Good enough."

I didn't understand the implications of all this, but there was no mistaking Donovan's meaning when he said, "Come on, kid, we're leaving. And don't give me any lip."

He backed out the door and I followed. There was nothing else I could do.

Once away from the cabin Donovan threw the shells from Hank and Emmitt's rifles into the brush. He looked at me and grumbled, "That was a cute trick you tried back there, but not very original. I don't know if you're worth the trouble of saving."

It took all the daylight hours to return and Donovan didn't speak once. Hour after hour he plodded ahead, the rifle slung over his back by a sling.

I followed behind. I became ravenously hungry and I wanted to rest. But anger and stubbornness were boiling in me and I'd have dropped before I'd let Donovan know.

We had finished supper and I was getting ready to clean up when Donovan said, "Sit down." It was an order.

I sat on my bunk and Donovan on the bench facing me.

"Did a lot of thinking on the way back," he began. "Don't blame you for wanting to get home and doing anything to get there. But you can't do it the way you tried and you can't do it now. You've got to wait. Am I going to have to chase you down every few days and bring you back, or are you through trying foolish stunts?"

The anger that had been building in me during the long hike back had smothered my fear of him. Now I found a courage and determination I hadn't known I possessed. I met Donovan's eyes squarely and said, "I don't know. Give me some good reasons I should believe you. I don't see much difference between you and Hank and Emmitt. You told Hank you were all up here for the same reasons. That if you cut each other to mincemeat you'd be saving the authorities in the south forty-eight the trouble of doing it. Just what did that mean? If I'm going to live here with you there's some things I want to know."

Donovan rubbed his chin and said, "Guess you're right. There isn't much difference between Hank and Emmitt and me and a few hundred others. All right, I'll bring you up to date.

"There's a lot of men up here that are wanted in the south forty-eight. Their crimes range from murder to you-name-it. They've managed to escape the police and come north, changed their names, and lost themselves in this more than half a million square miles of wilderness. The police know they're here somewhere, but it takes too long and costs too much to try to run them down and bring them to justice. Since they've divorced themselves from civilization, let them live out their lives up here. If they ever return, they'll be caught and prosecuted. The police down south don't care what happens to them."

"How many are there?"

"I've heard guesses. Around three hundred."

"You think Hank and Emmitt are two of them?"

"After last night I'd bet my life on it. They weren't taking you out, but were going to get rid of you."

"Why? They were getting three or four thousand."

"Bait money, to make it look like a legitimate deal. They were leading you further inland, away from people and any possible chance of help."

44

"But why?"

"Did you give them any hint that you suspected they might be wanted, or say anything that might arouse their suspicions? Did you tell them about your friend Ross and how you got stranded here?"

I nodded. "I didn't mention Ross. But the last time they were here I told them Dad was a criminal lawyer and if they had any trouble with the law he'd take their case if they got me out. Right off Emmitt was afraid. Hank thought about it but he said nothing."

"That could be it. They're as skittish and suspicious as the wildest animal. They probably figure your father could know about them. And he might. My guess is that if they're taken back, the penalty could be very stiff. On the other hand, and I'm not saying they had anything to do with it, they might know something about that trapper and whoever killed Ross. So they can't let you return down south because you could inform on them or draw unwanted attention to them. You're not exactly in an enviable position."

"What about this man who has short wave and can call out a plane to get me?"

"There may be such a man. I'm betting not."

"How do you think they planned to get rid of me?" I was surprised I could discuss my own elimination so calmly.

"They were leading you further away, inland, away from any people and the possibility of help. By tomorrow night they'd be so far away that, while you slept the sleep of exhaustion, they could take your parka and all the grub and leave. Naturally you'd follow their tracks back, but you'd never make it without your parka and food."

"Why not shoot me or knock me in the head and get it over with?"

"If they did, your body might be found in the spring and the police have ways of proving death, so why take that chance? This way, you'd have frozen to death. An accident. As far as anyone knows, you were lost anyway. They'd be home free. I'll bet that's how Hank figured it out."

It was hard to believe. But now that I knew the kind of men they were it made sense. I said, "I didn't help your case with them. I'm sorry."

"Confrontation with them was overdue."

Once again I found myself thinking of the odd enigma of this big, quiet, rawboned man. I didn't want to ask, but I'd been building up to it for days. I had to. "Mr. Donovan, why are you living up here this way? You're not a trapper. It's obvious you don't enjoy living the way you are. Are you one of the three hundred evading the law? What about you, Mr. Donovan?"

"How old did you say you are?"

"Almost eighteen."

"You're sharp and you're observant." He looked down at his hands and rasped them together thoughtfully. Then he met my eyes for a long moment. When he spoke his voice was rougher than I'd ever heard it. "I'm just like Hank and Emmitt. I'm one of those three hundred.

"We're all men with a past but no future. We live for today because there's no tomorrow. In my case, if you or somebody told the authorities where Mike Donovan could be found, I'd be taken back south to Washington where I'd be tried, and, undoubtedly, convicted and sent to prison for life or the gas chamber or hung. Whichever they do. So I exist up here one day at a time. This whole state is my prison because three years ago I killed a man." His big fists were clenched, his jaw set, and in his brown eyes there was a hopeless kind of misery I'd seen once before in my life. In my father's eyes the day Mother had died.

- 6 -

So this was what a murderer looked like. Smooth, weather-tanned brown skin, a rough hewn face with a square jaw, a lean, tough body, and a shadow of tragedy in his brown eyes I felt would never leave. The only thing I could think to say was, "I always felt you were no trapper. What were you before you came here?"

"You want to tell your dad how easy it'd be to run me down and take me back, eh?" The weak moment, if you could call it that, was gone. His voice was tough, impersonal again.

"Is that the way you think I'd pay you back for twice saving my life?" I said angrily. "You've got some things to learn, too, Mr. Donovan."

"Sorry," Donovan shook his head, "I had that coming. Living up here alone, thinking about it almost every day, you get pretty touchy. Man can think of some pretty wild things. What do you want to know?"

"Anything you'd care to tell me. I've been rather curious about you from the first day. If you'd rather not talk about it, fine. But anything you tell me is between you and me. Sometimes talking helps."

Donovan looked at the floor. He clasped and unclasped his big hands. Finally he sort of nodded and sighed. "Man can be alone too long. I've never told a living soul what happened — fact is there was no one to tell. I guess it's time I talked to somebody.

"I went into business with a lifelong friend. We had a little high-tech company. Made printed circuit boards among other things. It was a hand-to-mouth existence the first three or four years. Then we got a big break, an order for five million circuit boards for pocket calculators. We were on our way.

"Things went along fine the first year. Then I discovered this so-called friend and partner was robbing me blind and my wife of fifteen years was helping him. At first I couldn't believe it. I took a couple of months checking the company and watching my wife take off almost every night on some phony errand. She was meeting him. I got mad, and one night I went to his place for a showdown.

"I accused him of the whole thing and I didn't spare my wife. He pulled a gun and ordered me out. I knocked the gun out of his hand and we both went for it. I got it. I meant to throw it out the window and work him over with my fists. But he got his hand locked around mine. I couldn't throw the gun. We fought all over the room. The gun went off. The bullet went through his heart.

"I stood there holding the gun and with him lying on the floor, dead. The door opened and there was my wife. Her mouth was open as if she was about to scream and her eyes were bulging. I dropped the gun and got out fast."

"Didn't you talk to anyone about it?"

"There wasn't time. I knew the minute my wife could get to a phone the police would be knocking at the door. I toyed with the idea of giving myself up, but I knew I wouldn't have a chance in a trial. I had gone over there. My prints were all over the gun, the room. It would sure look premeditated. And my wife certainly wouldn't testify in my behalf. The whole thing was stacked against me. I didn't have a leg to stand on, and they were two people not worth going to prison or dying for.

"I headed north. I'd been up here hunting for several years and stayed with the old man who lived in this cabin. Charlie Wright was a trapper and miner. He's got quite a tunnel into the side of a hill a couple miles from here. He had died and the cabin was vacant. I moved in and here I am."

"What's happened to your company?"

He shrugged, "Folded, maybe, or sold."

I was surprised at the similarities between us. And the accusations Donovan had made when he refused to walk me out still rankled. Now I threw them back at him. "There's not much difference how you got up here and me."

"How do you mean?"

"You accused me of quitting in that fight with Scrapiron — and I did because I couldn't lick him. I ran away because I couldn't face up to the abuse my father would heap on me. I figured on returning in a couple of days and taking his tongue lashing. You ran away, too. You didn't put up any fight for your company, your wife, or yourself. You thought you didn't have a chance and you had a lot more to fight for than I did. You're a bigger quitter than I am. We both hit the panic button and ran. But I'm going back and face my father and it'll be a lot worse now than before because he'll add my running away to it. You don't ever plan to return."

"There's a world of difference between our reasons and you know it."

"The principle's the same."

"No way. I could go to prison for life, or to the gas chamber."

"You don't know that. You're still jumping to conclusions. You're still panicking."

"You haven't been listening, kid." He was half angry. "I killed a man. Get that through your head."

"And you're not listening or thinking very straight." I tried to think as my father would if he were building a defense. "It could have been self-defense. You were fighting over the gun. He threatened you with it. It was his gun, so you didn't run over there with one. Also, he was robbing your company."

"Some of that might be hard to prove. I went to his place for a showdown. The fact he was robbing me and my wife was in collusion could be construed as reason for killing him."

"Do you know your wife was helping him?"

"She was there. It wasn't the first time."

"That's not proof she was working against you."

"Then why was she meeting him night after night?"

"Ever heard of collecting evidence? Maybe she was trying to get facts that would help you."

Donovan shook his head, "Wishful thinking. A good lawyer would twist those facts so I looked guilty as sin."

"And another good lawyer could twist them so you looked innocent."

"All right — suppose I go back, and in a trial I lose. The police have got me."

"There's appeal. A trial for a murder conviction always carries an appeal."

"Suppose I lose the appeal?"

"You're taking it for granted you will lose. I'm not."

"The fact that I'd lost once would mean I'd be taking a big chance on the second," Donovan said thoughtfully. "Up here at least, I'm free."

"Are you? Can you go to the city or any town and walk down the street in broad daylight? Can you, safely, walk into any store or building?"

"You know I can't."

"You enjoy living year after year in this cabin, walking around on the same tundra, playing tag with wolves, bears, and moose?"

"You know I don't."

"Then you're not free. The bars are just too far away to see. If you don't do something to fight back, this's how you'll spend the next twenty-five or thirty years. You've got the rest of your life to fight for."

"You think I haven't thought about this a hundred times?"

"Then do something about it. Look at the possibilities for once. If you take this lying down, you're a bigger quitter than I am."

"I prefer to call myself a survivalist," Donovan said stiffly.

"That's the worst kind of alibi."

"Didn't you say you wanted to become a lawyer?"

"Yes."

"You'll make a good one. Let's call it quits, it's been a long day."

In the days that followed, I no longer stayed near the fire pile and watched the sky for a search plane. I'd given up any hope of one coming.

Almost daily Donovan took off across the flat tundra carrying his rifle. He seldom returned with game. After that one night when we'd talked, he had returned to the quiet, morose, uncommunicative man I'd first known. He spoke of that evening's discussion of his problem once. It was almost a week later. He sat staring at the floor, big fingers laced together, expression thoughtful. Finally he said, "Been thinking about what you said the other night. You really believe my wife was trying to help me?"

"It's possible. I'm sure Dad would think so, too."

"Sounds logical when you talk. It doesn't when I think about it." He was silent for a little, then, "Sometimes you can be alone too much. Your thinking gets in a rut. It takes somebody else to sort of jar you out of it and see there can be another side to a problem."

I said, "You're still in love with your wife, aren't you?"

"We were married fifteen years. Good ones, I thought."

"You'd be surprised what Dad could find for a defense. He's a digger. He works for his client. I've known him to win cases other lawyers wouldn't touch."

"Should have known your dad." He rolled over on his bunk. "Turn out the light when you're ready."

A few minutes later I blew out the light and crawled into my sleeping bag. Donovan's voice came to me out of the dark, "I hit the panic button all right, but I figured I had the best of reasons. I wanted to live."

I thought about that and listened to the night sounds of this primitive land. The soft scrape of a branch across the logs. The knife-edge voice of a night bird. The small firecracker-like explosion as the intense cold popped a log.

Donovan was right. Compared to his reasons for running, mine were silly, childish. For the first time I admitted I should have taken Dad's tongue lashing. It wouldn't have been so bad and I had it coming. Then I should have hunted up Scrapiron and finished that fight. I'd probably have lost, but I could have come away with a little pride. I could even see where Dad had a point in his yelling. If I backed away from every tough problem I met, I wouldn't make much of a lawyer or anything else. I hoped this facing up to some of my own shortcomings while lying on a pole bunk in a log cabin somewhere in the frigid Arctic meant I was growing up a little.

The sub-zero days slipped away. Wind and an all night snowstorm covered my fire pile. I didn't bother to clear the snow off it. I puttered about the cabin trying to think of things to do. There wasn't much. I'd read all the novels that interested me. I reread the Robert Service poems I liked best, memorizing a few parts. I even read long sections of the desk encyclopedia and looked up the meanings of words in the dictionary. I would have liked to go out on the tundra with Donovan but the big man didn't invite me. He did mention once that we'd have to get another moose soon or stop feeding the wolves.

There was plenty of time to think and I did a lot of that. I was learning things about myself and the North during those lonely days.

Out here on the tundra, civilization's thinking and manner of living hadn't taken hold. Life was simpler, slower. In this land of long nights, few people, and cold-induced death, you got down to basics in a hurry if you wanted to live. Eating, starving, living, dying, love, hate, greed. There was no in-between. My thinking, I came to realize, had slipped back to the days of the great Klondike gold rush, the Chilkoot Pass, and travel only on foot or by dog team.

The wolves provided the high point of my days. Regardless of the weather, they came. I watched for them and they arrived almost on the minute. They'd come trotting through the brush, Blackie always in the lead, Fawn close behind, tails waving expectantly. They sat silently side by side in front of the cabin and patiently waited for me to appear.

Thoughts of Hank and Emmitt and Hank's threat hurled at Donovan bothered me. But days passed and nothing happened. I pushed it into the back of my mind until the day I spotted a figure cutting into a ravine about half a mile from the cabin. It looked like Hank's big, skulking shape. I slipped into my parka and went out to check.

Donovan walked out of the ravine, his rifle over his arm. I told him what I'd suspected. "I guess that crack you gave him on the head taught him a lesson. We haven't seen hide nor hair of them since."

"Don't fool yourself," Donovan said roughly. "Hank's afraid of no one. That night he dove into me right under the muzzle of the rifle. That took nerve. I was lucky. A second slower I wouldn't have nailed him." He added thoughtfully, "I'll bet that was the first time anybody ever dropped him. He'll be sure it doesn't happen again."

"You really think Hank's that dangerous?"

"Hank can't be bluffed. He's a vicious, dangerous man. So's Emmitt. But Hank's the leader, he's the one." Donovan was silent a moment, staring off into the white distance, "One thing I'm sure of now, they're part of some gang down south."

"What makes you sure?" I asked.

"When I cracked Hank over the head he said, 'If you knew who I was down south, you'd know I don't bluff.' That was a dead giveaway."

I remembered the savage look on Hank's face, the deadly coldness in his black eyes, and the words came voluntarily, "I've never seen a gangster. You think they're—what do they call them—hit men?"

Donovan rubbed snow from the rifle barrel. "They could be a lot of things. Hit men is only one. But it doesn't make sense. Gangs have a way of protecting their hit men who get in trouble with the law. They don't have to send them clear up here. But what else could a couple of gang men do that would call for something as severe as this banishment?

"I like logical explanations, and with Hank and Emmitt there aren't any. Anyway," he shrugged, "it's none of my business. I just don't like riddles." He turned to leave, then looked back at me, "Keep away from those two, you've had enough trouble with them. Just remember, whether they wear expensive suits and shoes or parkas and boots and look like disreputable trappers, underneath they're cold blooded and vicious and they know their business." With that he stalked off toward the cabin.

- 7 -

I had hoped with the passing of time my relationship with this big, impassive, moody man would find some common ground. But we remained practically strangers, living together in this small cabin, scarcely communicating. Again and again I tried to strike up conversations with him. I racked my brain trying to dredge up some subject that would interest him. But if he was skinning an animal, he continued as if he hadn't heard. Or if he was sitting, doing nothing, he continued to scowl at the floor or his hands and grunted a reply that killed my efforts. Finally, I gave up and went my own way.

Without the wolves I don't know what I'd have done. I could talk to them. They were alive. For that short time I could forget my loneliness and this bleak, unfriendly land.

Fawn was easy to play with and I enjoyed our romps. I loved to watch how her tail snapped as she lunged through the flying snow, dodging my clumsy rushes at her, the breathy little barks of sheer joy, the way she stood and studied me, ears erect, pink tongue lolling in a wolfish grin, sharp eyes waiting my next move.

Blackie ignored all my advances. The big wolf sat on his tail and watched, inscrutable as a sphinx, no expression, no warmth or interest. But those direct, sharp eyes took in every move Fawn and I made.

I tried everything to include Blackie in our play. I walked slowly toward him, hand out, talking softly, "Come on, there's no reason you and I can't be friends. Fawn and I are. I'm not going to hurt you, that's for sure, and you're not going to hurt me." But when I crossed his invisible line, he backed away. I even tried running at him playfully, careful not to cross the line, but Blackie simply sat and looked at me.

One day, after trying particularly hard and getting nowhere, I said, half angrily, "Come off it, Blackie. You're not half as smart as you'd like me to believe. I once knew a judge who acted just like you. He sat up there on the bench in his black robe and looked and listened and never smiled and hardly ever spoke. He looked severe and impressive. I asked Dad once if he was as smart as he looked. Dad just shrugged and said, 'He doesn't give you much chance to find out.'" Blackie sat and watched me, his ears focused on my voice.

Fawn ran out her pink tongue, barked inquisitively, and gave me her grin. "You like him, eh? Well, there's no accounting for taste." I tossed them their slabs of moose meat and watched them trot away. Tails high. Blackie in the lead.

Each day before the wolves arrived, I'd read for a while, trying to drive boredom away by testing my memory. Most days, after the wolves had disappeared and Donovan had been gone for hours, I hiked out across the tundra just to look at the land and whatever animals I might see. Finally, that, too, became boring.

Then I began to imagine things that could happen. I'd given up on a plane or chopper coming. But a dog team or snowmobile could come streaking across this flat land. Maybe they'd quit searching with planes and were using dog teams and sleds since it was winter.

A man, or several men, could come slogging through the snow on a search. Or maybe some trapper who could help me. I wanted to get away from Donovan and this frozen land so bad I even considered hunting up Hank and Emmitt again and trying to make another deal to take me out. After all, I reasoned, I only had Donovan's word for it that they were vicious characters from some gang down south — that they had planned to lose me that other time so I'd die of exposure. That, I reasoned, was a pretty far-fetched conclusion, especially for a man who'd admitted he'd killed someone who'd been his friend and partner. Then I'd remember Hank's black eyes boring into me and the uncomfortable, wary feeling it always gave me. And last, there was the night Donovan caught up with us and crashed the rifle barrel against Hank's head. The murderous look on Hank's face had sent a chill through me. I discarded the idea. There was also what had happened to Ross to consider. Somebody had meant to destroy the plane, even if they didn't know anyone was in it. I was stuck here the rest of the winter with a man who was as cold and impersonal as the climate.

During these hikes I thought often of home and my father and Rocky and particularly the lack of warmth and closeness with Dad. Maybe if I'd waded into Scrapiron and taken a terrific beating it might have changed things. But I doubted it. There'd never been anything special between us like there was with Rocky. He'd probably have slapped me on the back and said, "Nice going. You made a fight of it." For that small praise I'd have taken a couple of real beatings. No way!

One day, wrapped in these thoughts and feeling particularly low and lonesome, I went further than I intended. It was an odd, half-dark day. I was walking under a gray, leaden-colored sky that seemed to hang about fifty feet above the snow. It was deathly still. I saw no game of any kind. I was so steeped in my own misery that I heard the sound for several minutes before it registered on my mind. Then I looked up. There, sweeping across the flat tundra just under the cloud bank and coming straight toward me, was a helicopter.

I froze. I had dreamed of it happening so many times just like this. It had to be a dream. I blinked my eyes hard. I rubbed them. The helicopter was still there.

The chopper came lower. It was over me! It kicked up clouds of snow almost blinding me. Sound and wind beat at me. The face of the pilot was staring down. Just below the lowering clouds it circled me. In another moment it would settle on the snow. This was it! The impossible dream was coming true right before my eyes. I waved in frantic welcome. The pilot waved back.

Home! I was going home! They had found me at last! The nightmare was over. My eyes blurred. My heart was suddenly too big for my chest.

The chopper made two complete circles, then it straightened and with a long low swoop flew straight away.

It couldn't be! It couldn't! I let out a throat-tearing scream, "Down here! I'm down here! Come back! Come back!"

Still close to the ground and no more than a quarter mile away the chopper began making wide sweeps to right and left apparently searching for something. The pilot had seen me. Why hadn't he landed? Why?

I began to run through the crusty snow still shouting at the top of my lungs. I tripped and fell, scrambled up and ran again. I kept my eyes on the chopper. Its wide right and left swings made it draw away slowly. The frigid air brought tears to my eyes and tore like a knife into my lungs. But still I ran.

I left the flat, open tundra and entered an area of scrub brush and trees. Here the chopper was harder to see and at times for minutes it was lost to sight. But I still heard the beat of the rotor blades.

It came into sight again, hovering in the air. Then it dropped and was hidden by the brush. The sound of the blades stopped. It had landed.

I kept running. Tears streamed down my face, my lungs were on fire — but my legs kept churning.

I rounded a patch of brush and there was a cabin with the chopper sitting in front of it. It was Hank and Emmitt's! The pilot stood a few feet away from me, his back to me. Hank and Emmitt were emerging from the cabin, each carrying a huge bale of fur. The bales they carried were so big they hid their faces and they couldn't see me. I dove behind a thick clump of brush and lay half-hidden in the foot-deep snow.

I was no more than a hundred feet from the cabin and in the dead silence I could even hear the squeak of their feet in the dry snow.

The pilot said, "I'll leave this batch with the other in the old cabin. You fellows about through here?"

"Just about," Hank said. "We better leave pretty soon before somebody begins askin' questions."

"Yeah," Emmitt said, "with all we got we better pull stakes."

The pilot got into the chopper and started the motor, then he yelled out the open door, "Seen a guy back a ways. He was comin' this way. Anybody you might know?"

"Could be," Hank answered. "We'll check him out."

The pilot slammed the door and the chopper lifted into the air.

Once the chopper noise faded I heard Hank say, "Somebody headed this way, huh. We've got to check him out. It'll be Donovan or th' kid, and I'm bettin' on th' kid. We got to check him out right now." They disappeared inside the cabin — I knew why — to get guns.

I jumped up and ran. I followed my tracks back. I knew they'd be right behind me — following my tracks. There was no way I could hide. My only hope was to outrun them and reach the safety of Donovan's cabin — Donovan and his big rifle.

There was a single shot behind me. Ten feet ahead snow jumped off a limb where the bullet had hit. They were out of range and shooting while running. It would be sheer luck if they hit me. But I had to be far enough ahead so that when I reached the spot where my tracks led out into the open tundra I'd be well beyond the range of their rifles.

A few minutes later my tracks cut straight out of the brush. I stopped and glanced back, but through the tangled limbs I could not see them. I looked across the two miles of flat, treeless, brushless snow that led to Donovan's cabin. A gust of wind picked up the snow and swirled it about. It raced toward me, cut to my right and entered the brush shaking snow from the limbs. A couple more little twisters had formed and were skipping about. Snow particles glistened in the air and stung my face. I dared not charge into the open. Hank and Emmitt would soon be in rifle range, and on that flat snow even a rabbit would be visible. I had to abandon my tracks back to the cabin and stick to the brush. I looked at the sky. Dark would soon be here. Until then I had to stay in the brush and keep running. In the dark I could sneak back, cross that flat and get to the cabin.

I ran again, keeping to the brush. I entered an area that was strange to me. I stopped to catch my breath and looked around. The brush here was thicker, the trees bigger. I glanced back as a single shot knifed the silence. Snow bounced from a limb five feet to one side. I glimpsed Hank dodging through the brush. The bullet had gone wild because he'd shot while running.

For a moment I simply stood there. No one had ever shot at me before. "Hank's trying to scare me," I told myself. But I knew better. Hank would never shoot to scare. He meant to hit what he shot at. I began running again.

Running in a foot of snow is like running in so much water. You can do it for a short distance, but you tire fast. My legs were still weary from my first frantic dash after the chopper. I had to stop to catch my breath, then run again.

A wind and snow whirlwind suddenly enveloped me, stinging my face and blinding me. I stopped and waited for it to pass. It didn't pass. I pulled the parka hood closer around my face to protect my face and eyes. The wind whistled and clawed at me. The brush waved and snapped and cracked. I tried to shield my eyes with my mittened hands. My world had suddenly closed down to a few feet of driving snow and cutting wind.

I turned my back and tried to back into it, but it seemed to come from all directions. Behind me my tracks were already filling in. In a few minutes there would be no tracks. All about me snow whipped across the frozen earth filling every nook and cranny, covering every stick and grass clump that lay exposed. The very breath seemed torn out of my lungs. Wind cut through the heavy parka and drove the heat from my body. I had to find some sort of protection in a hurry.

I backed into something solid. I turned. A tree had fallen and I was right up against a wall of roots. I felt my way around the mass and into a protected hole. I squeezed into it as far as I could. It formed a kind of eddy and the bulk of the wind and snow swirled around and over me.

In here wind no longer cut through the parka, and my face and eyes were protected from the driving snow. I'd never been in any kind of blizzard. I was alone. I could freeze to death here — and Hank and Emmitt could come out of this driving snow any minute. I raised up and looked about for them. Then I noticed my tracks were almost drifted over. In a few more minutes there'd be no trace of them.

I began to reason then. Hank and Emmitt must have lost my trail by now and were hunting me blind — if they were hunting at all. If I'd been blinded, so had they. If I was freezing, so were they. I was years younger and in better shape to take this than they were. I bet they were headed back for their cabin. I really had nothing to worry about but this storm. In a few minutes I was actually reasonably warm. I wondered how long this storm would last — a day, two days — Donovan couldn't possibly find me without tracks to follow. I meant to wait out this storm however long it took. I was hungry. I was going to get a lot hungrier, but I could last it out.

I burrowed deeper into the snow and curled up like pictures I'd seen of Alaskan sled dogs sleeping in the snow. My thoughts drifted off to home, to Rocky and Dad. I wondered vaguely what they'd think if they knew I'd been shot at and chased by a pair of men intent on killing me. That I was now hiding buried deep in the snow while a blizzard roared over and around me somewhere in the wilds of Alaska. Mostly I wondered how they'd have handled this situation — no better than I was, I bet. Thinking of that was a most satisfying feeling.

Surprisingly, I dozed off. I awoke suddenly and listened to the whistling wind and looked at the whirling snow building a wall around me. I dozed again. That happened several times. The rim of snow built higher around me and I was snug and warm.

It must have been hours later that I came fully awake. The first thing I was conscious of was a silence so complete I could almost hear it. The storm was over. I stood up and shook the snow off me. The sky had a soft, blue look. The stars were out. Dawn was not far off. The snow was piled up inches deeper. My tracks were completely gone. Hank and Emmitt would not come looking for me now. I was so hungry my stomach felt tied in knots. I had to find Donovan's cabin.

I began hiking back searching for the spot where I'd first seen the chopper. But I'd paid no attention to brush or rocks and of course my prints were wiped out. The land was one great, white, unbroken expanse with no identifying marks whatever. How far, I wondered, had I followed the chopper from the point I'd first seen it to Hank and Emmitt's cabin? A half mile — a mile? How far had I run from their cabin with them chasing me? Another mile — two miles? I tried to guess the time, the speed I'd been traveling to keep ahead of them. I hadn't the faintest idea. I cut back into the brush searching for a clue of any kind that would give me some indication of where I was. If there was anything, it was hidden beneath the snow. All the days before when I hiked about I paid little attention to where I went. I could always follow my tracks back. Now there were none. Everything looked at once familiar and strange.

Standing on the fringe of the brush I looked all about. Gradually it came to me that I was lost. I remembered something I'd read or heard, "When you're lost, any direction you choose to get out of trouble is always the wrong one. You simply become more lost."

I left the brush and walked out into the flat, open tundra for several hundred yards, looking for something, anything that would give me direction. A moose came to the edge of the brush, looked at me, turned back, and disappeared. I thought of Donovan. Surely he'd come looking for me. But how would he know which direction to take?

I was about to head straight across that open tundra and if I found nothing, I could follow my tracks back to the brush again. I was debating that move when a movement at the edge of the brush caught my eye. The next moment Blackie and Fawn walked into the open. Blackie was leading, breaking trail, and Fawn was right behind. They saw me and stopped.

I was as happy to see them as if they were a couple of humans. "Blackie, Fawn," I called, "boy, am I glad to see you!"

Fawn recognized my voice. She grinned and began waving her tail. Blackie dropped his big head and gave me that direct stare as if he was measuring me for a charge. I spoke directly to him, "Oh, come off it, you're not kidding anybody. You know me. I feed you moose steaks every day." I started toward them holding out my hand, talking softly, intimately. "How many steaks have I fed you guys? You wait for me every day right outside the cabin. You're about the biggest moocher I've ever seen. Are you heading for the cabin now? By the time you get there it'll be just about time for your lunch.

"I'm lost. I mean really lost. You know what it's like to be lost? Believe me, it's scary. You wouldn't know about that. This's your home. If you're heading for the cabin, I'm going with you. I'm hungry, I'm tired, and I'm scared, too. Come on, guys, take me home."

Fawn kept waving her tail and grinning at me. Her sharp ears jumped back and forth catching every inflection in my voice. Blackie just looked at me, inscrutable, calm, dignified.

When I reached the usual distance they allowed me, Blackie turned and started walking away. Fawn followed in his tracks. I let them get a hundred yards or so ahead, then I dropped in behind.

Breaking trail was tough going for Blackie. The snow was almost chest deep but he plowed straight ahead. Fawn was close behind following exactly in his tracks. It made walking easy for me. We must have made an odd picture — two wolves and a man traveling across the tundra in single file.

I was sure Blackie was heading the wrong way, but I was lost and he seemed to know where he was going. I made no attempt to stay close to them.

The wolves kept to a steady pace but I had to stop several times to rest. I kept a sharp lookout for tracks in the hope Donovan would be out looking for me. But there was nothing to break the utter smoothness of the snow. I tried to tell myself it was a big land. He could be hunting some other direction, but we should have crossed his tracks at least once or twice. Gradually a smoldering anger built up in me. Donovan was cold, emotionless, uncaring. If he were lost I'd try to find him. But not Donovan. He didn't care if I froze or starved to death. In fact, he'd probably be glad to get rid of me.

We followed the edge of the brush for some time and then the wolves cut out straight across the open tundra. Finally they breasted a long, gentle rise that somehow looked a little familiar and disappeared over the top. When I reached the top, Blackie was a small, black blob almost half a mile away. Fawn blended so well with the play of light and shadows on the snow, I could barely make her out. They were plugging ahead at the same tireless pace. They came to a finger of brush that reached into the flat tundra and disappeared.

When I finally rounded the brush patch, there, two hundred yards away, sat the cabin with a trail of smoke roping from the tin smoke stack. I was so disoriented and lost that for a moment I didn't recognize it, but there were Fawn and Blackie sitting on their tails before the door as they always did. I broke into a run. Never had anyplace looked so good.

When I opened the door, Donovan was at the stove getting lunch. He had a moose steak in the pan and was frying it. The two braids of long hair hung down each side of his head and once again he looked like pictures of Indians I'd seen. When I saw the food I realized I must have been wandering around at least five hours.

He glanced at me and said bluntly, "So, you decided to come back."

I looked at him bent over the stove calmly cooking while I'd been slogging through the snow, lost, half-frozen, and frightened. "Decided!" I shot at him angrily.

"Exactly," he said. "When I got back you were gone and you didn't show and didn't show. Just like it was that first time when you made the deal with Hank and Emmitt behind my back. I was lucky then and caught up with you before they could do you harm."

I just stared at him speechless.

"If that's what you wanted," he continued, "and were willing to take the chance with them when you knew what they were.... Okay. You're old enough to know what you're doing. I wasn't going to chase after you again. Once was enough."

"For your information," I yelled at him, "I got lost and Hank and Emmitt chased me and shot at me. The only thing that saved me from them was that blizzard that drifted my tracks shut and blinded them so they couldn't see me." Then my anger spilled over at this big emotionless, impersonal, cold man. "I don't like you. I didn't from the first time I saw you. I'd have tried Hank and Emmitt again if they could get me away from you. But if you'd been out there lost, maybe freezing to death and chased by Hank and Emmitt as I was, I'd have tried to help you. But not you, oh no, you hung around the cabin glowering at the stove or something while I was freezing and dodging bullets.

"If Fawn and Blackie hadn't happened along and brought me back, maybe I'd be dead by now and you'd be rid of me. You're no better than Hank and Emmitt, you just tried to kill me differently."

I'd run out of words. I just stood there glaring at him, fists clenched. For the first time in my life, I think, I wanted to get even with someone. I wanted to hurt Donovan. I wanted to hurt him bad. Then I saw the haunch of moose meat lying on the table. He loved the wolves. He was about to feed them as he'd been doing for two years until I came and had taken over doing it part of the time.

I grabbed the knife, "I'm going to feed the wolves. But for them I wouldn't be here now." I hacked off two huge chunks and stomped out of the cabin slamming the door.

Even as I was doing it I knew it was a childish kind of rebellion, a silly sort of way of getting even. But I had to do something and at the moment depriving him of feeding the wolves was the only thing I could think of.

I went carefully, as always, talking to them all the way. "Here you are," I said. "You'll never know how glad I was to see you this morning. I wish you could understand what I'm saying so I could thank you properly. I'm sorry, this is the best I can do, but maybe these steaks will mean more to you than any words. You sure earned them. But for you I'd have died out there. I'd like to give you a real banquet, but I don't think you'd care for the kind I'm thinking of. I'll never forget what you did for me." Fawn waved her tail and lifted her lips in a grin. Blackie's ears shot forward and he studied me, and I felt he was taking in every inflection in my voice. I tossed the meat toward them, "Here you are, my friends. Good eating." I watched them trot off into the brush, heads high, tails waving. Then I turned back to the cabin.

Inside, Donovan pushed me down on the bunk, then sat opposite me on the bench. He handed me a small bottle capped and sealed and filled with matches. "Now," he asked, "you got a knife?"

I said, surprised, "Just a little pocket knife, why?"

He handed me a heavy folding knife with about a six-inch blade. "Now put those two in the pocket of your parka. Never be without them. If you ever get lost again they can save your life. You understand that. Never be without them. Never!

"Now, about my not coming to look for you. I made a mistake, a very bad mistake, but I did think you'd gone over to Hank and Emmitt's. But forget that, I want the whole story from the time you left the cabin yesterday to this morning. And what's this about them shooting at you?"

So I told him all the things that had happened since I left the cabin yesterday. He sat, arms folded, looking straight at me, those brown eyes telling me nothing. He interrupted a few times with sharp questions.

"The pilot seemed to know where he was going?"

"Yes, and when he loaded the furs he told them he'd put it with their others."

Donovan nodded, "Then the pilot didn't just happen to come out. They called him. Which means they've got a short wave. That tell you something?" he asked.

"Yes. They weren't taking me to another trapper further inland who had one. They were going to do just what you said. Get rid of me."

"I've wondered all along what they were doing out here. They're robbing other trappers of their catches. And they've evidently killed at least one and maybe more. Probably the guy you and Ross were delivering to. And Ross."

"I thought about that when they were hunting me. Would stealing furs pay?" I asked.

"Sure. Some trappers have lines that take a week or more to get around. They go in with thousands of dollars worth come spring. I know a couple further up in the hills who do very well. One of them disappeared a few months ago. The pilot who brings out my grub and takes in my fur was wondering why he left a fine trapline."

"You think Hank and Emmitt killed him for his fur and what I saw was part of his catch?"

"I'd bet on it. That little line of theirs is just a screen for what they're really doing. I'll bet they've killed a couple of trappers to get that much fur to load a chopper."

Donovan studied me soberly until it began to bother me and I asked, "Is anything wrong?"

He nodded, "They know now you saw them loading that fur. They've probably guessed you came on the plane, so you might know about that trapper and Ross. The fact they chased you and shot at you is proof they can't let you get back to civilization where you can inform on them."

"What makes them think I would?"

"Kid, don't act so stupid," he said harshly. "You ought to be able to figure that out, but I'll draw you a picture. You're an honest, respectable kid. It's your duty to inform the police of anything illegal. On top of that, your dad's a lawyer. Naturally they'd expect you to tell him and he'd take it from there. You tell your dad or the authorities and it can open a whole can of worms. There's no telling how many other crimes they've committed. They're worried and probably scared. They've got to be jumping at shadows now. You be mighty careful how you go ramming around the country from now on. Stay in the open and keep your eyes peeled. Any human you see will be them or me. You don't want it to be them. They've got to think you're the most dangerous person in the world to them — and they're dead right."

66

- 8 -

The realization that I was dangerous to anyone — dangerous enough to be killed — hung over me like some mad nightmare. For several days I did not venture outside the cabin except to feed the wolves. I fed them, and Fawn charged circles around me inviting me to play, but my heart wasn't in it.

Donovan gave no indication that Hank and Emmitt's attempt to kill me bothered him. But then, I told myself, he was a murderer, too. Each day he took off as usual and was gone most of the daylight hours. He did warn me repeatedly about being careful, and he asked several times if I'd seen anything of Hank and Emmitt.

Those first days I kept glancing out the half-open door, searching the tundra, half expecting to see them coming toward the cabin. I didn't even venture outside to feed the wolves until I'd stood in the open door long enough to inspect every close hillock, bush, and mound.

But the passing days dulled the sharp edge of the shock and I finally ventured forth again. This time I carried a light rifle. I'd never fired a rifle, yet just having it in my hands gave me a sense of security. But I soon learned it was the wolves themselves I trusted most. If they were sitting calmly in front of the cabin when I emerged, then everything was all right. I kept carefully out in the open. I came to know every bush, log, rock, and stump within a radius of several miles. And I kept a special lookout for human tracks that went in pairs.

Once I was startled when a moose heaved to its feet in front of me and went crashing away. I jerked up the rifle, my heart climbing into my throat. Then I just stood there and watched him disappear. A fox eating a rabbit startled me when I suddenly came upon it. A flock of ptarmigans exploded out of the snow under my feet and I almost yelled in fright.

But fear, when nothing happens to justify it, cannot last forever. Within a week I was back to feeding the wolves and playing with Fawn and trying to get Blackie to join in.

I returned early one afternoon and passed my old fire pile. It was almost fully hidden under the fall of snow. I was standing there debating whether I should tear it apart and burn the wood in the stove when the shot smashed across the tundra silence like a whiplash. There was just the one shot. Donovan must have killed the moose he'd been talking about to replenish our meat supply.

I went into the cabin and built up the fire to have it warm when he arrived. I waited and waited. Then I remembered it took time to skin out a big moose and Donovan could use help carrying in the meat. I closed the damper on the stove and headed out toward the sound of the shot.

About a mile from the cabin I came upon Fawn lying in the snow and Blackie standing guard beside her still form. There was blood on the snow near her front legs.

I said, "Fawn, oh Fawn!" and started towards her. Blackie dropped his head, a growl rumbled in his chest, and his lips lifted.

I slowed down but continued walking toward him. I began talking to him in a quiet, soothing voice. "All right. All right. Just take it easy. I know you want to protect her. I want to help her, too. She's hurt. You know me. I feed you moose steaks every day."

Blackie kept looking at me. His big head sank almost to the snow. His whole body seemed to draw together as if about to spring. Once again I had the prickly feeling he was measuring me for a lightning attack. My throat was dry. I was afraid my voice would give away my fear. But my tone remained calm, even. I kept moving forward. I got closer than I'd ever been to Blackie and his growls became deeper, harsher, more menacing. I was about to stop when he began backing away a slow step at a time. I kept the same line of quiet, pleading talk going, the same deliberate advance until I reached Fawn's side. The moment I stopped so did Blackie.

I dropped on my knees in the snow beside her. Her eyes were closed. I touched her shoulder and found her body warm, but there was no sign that she lived. I sat there stroking her soft fur and trying not to cry. I kept seeing her standing and laughing at me, her pink tongue hanging out, chasing me around in circles, cocking her head and studying me. Finally I began wondering what I should do. I couldn't leave her out here where scavengers would tear her apart. But I couldn't dig a grave in this iron-hard earth. And there were no rocks handy to build a cairn. I was still debating what to do when she opened her eyes and looked at me. She didn't try to move, just looked at me with those big golden eyes. Her chest rose and fell on a shuddering breath. She was alive!

I spoke her name, "Oh Fawn," I said. "Who shot you?" But I knew. Hank! It couldn't be anyone else. But why? Why?

Blackie stood about twenty feet away watching me. He cocked his head one way then the other as if trying to understand. He was no longer growling and showing his teeth.

I had to get her back to the cabin. I looked around for a couple of old, thick limbs I could put her on to pull her. There was nothing near I could use. If I only had the small sled Donovan had used to bring back the supplies from my wreck. There wasn't time to go to the cabin for it. I'd have to carry her.

I worked my hands carefully under her shoulders and hips and lifted. She whimpered. I got my hands further under her, cradled her in my arms, and tried again. She was heavier than I'd expected. She whimpered again but I got her against my chest, rose, and started back. Blackie watched me for a moment, then rose and began to follow.

It was hard tramping through more than a foot of snow trying to carry her carefully so I'd not jar her. A couple of times I stumbled and she whimpered. I stopped often to rest, and Blackie, following like a dog, stopped also. It must have taken the better part of an hour to reach the cabin.

I spread the hides that cushioned my bunk in a corner and laid her on them. Then I built up the fire and put a pan of snow on the stove to melt. With warm water and a rag I sponged off the bloody bullet hole. I was surprised how small it was. I wanted to turn her over to clean the exit hole, but she cried so piteously I gave up. I tried to give her a drink, but she just lay there, her eyes closed, breathing labored and shallow. I wanted to do more, but I felt helpless. I sat and stroked her sleek coat and talked softly to her and hoped Donovan would soon return.

When Donovan came in he said, "I heard a shot. Blackie's sitting out there...." Then he saw Fawn. He put the rifle down and knelt beside me. He touched Fawn gently and said in a voice I had never heard, "Easy, Baby. Easy." He looked at the bullet hole, felt her chest, her nose, pulled her eyelid up and looked at her eye. Then he said quietly, "Hank." It was a statement. "Where'd you find her?"

"About a mile straight out from the cabin. But why?" I asked. "If Hank wanted to get even with you or me, why shoot Fawn?"

"Hank's a sadistic character. Most of these crooks are. He's letting us know how easy he can take us. He wants us to worry. That's salve to his ego which is all important to him. It's what he lives on. He's always got to be top dog. The tough guy everybody's afraid of. He knows how we both feel about Fawn and Blackie. This is one way he can hurt us, try to keep us worried and afraid of him. One of his ways of getting even with me for that crack on the head I gave him."

I asked, "Is Fawn going to die?"

"I don't know. The bullet hole is high on the shoulder. If it'd been through the chest she'd be dead. There's no telling what damage it did inside. Have you looked at her other side, where it exited?"

"It hurt too much to turn her."

"We've got to look."

She whimpered and cried, but we turned her. The exit hole was much bigger and still oozed blood. Donovan trimmed the hair around it, washed it, and taped a clean cloth over it. "Hole seems to be clean," he said. "I can't tell if any bones are broken. It was a small caliber rifle. That's in her favor." He studied her a minute, then shook his head. "I don't know. Wolves are mighty tough animals, but that's a very bad place to be hit."

"What do we do — just wait?"

"I wouldn't say that."

An iron toughness in his voice made me look up. Donovan was standing, big fists clenched, craggy face set and ugly, his lips thinned down and tight. Then he reached for his rifle and a cold wind blew through me.

I asked, "What're you going to do?"

"Think I'll pay Hank and Emmitt a visit."

"You go over there you're apt to be killed."

"I'll be careful."

"There'll be a fight."

"That depends on them."

"Then there'll be a fight," I said.

"I haven't any choice. This was done deliberately to challenge me, not you. If they can control me, I'll keep you in line. They know Fawn is the only friend I've had up here in three years. Hank's testing me to see just how far he can go. If I let him get away with this it'll be just the beginning. Next they might burn us out. That would be as final as putting a gun to our heads. What I do tonight could keep us from being killed later."

I rose, slipped into my parka, and reached for a rifle. "I'm going with you."

"What do you think you can do?"

"I don't know. Neither do you."

"This's for real. These are mighty tough men, not kids. You should know that."

"I do know it. Hank shot at me, remember."

"Then you know it's no place for you."

I shook my head, "That's why I know it is."

"You're not used to guns. I can tell by the way you handle that one. I'll be wondering every minute what you're doing with it. You'll distract me — get in my way."

"I won't get in your way. I'm going."

Donovan jerked the gun from my hands. "You're staying if I have to tie you."

I looked straight into Donovan's stormy eyes. My fists were doubled, my chin up. It had to be to meet his eyes because he was taller. For the first time in my life I was challenging someone — a man — a bigger, tougher one than I. "You'll have to do it, then," I said. And I meant every word.

Donovan just looked at me. I could see surprise and something else that could have been the faint beginning of a smile. "Fawn means as much to me as she does to you," I continued. "She's the only friend I've had up here. Without her I don't know how I'd have made it this long. But there's a bigger reason: You said I was the most dangerous person in the world to them because I'd seen too much and I'll be leaving in the spring. So I'm going with you to try to make sure nothing happens to you. How long do you think I'd last up here alone with those two?"

Donovan seemed to turn that over in his mind then he nodded, "All right. But no rifle and don't interfere with me in any way. That understood?"

"I won't," I said. "But if I can help, I will."

Donovan felt Fawn's nose, patted her gently, and murmured, "You hold down the fort till we get back." Then he blew out the light and we left.

Night had claimed the tundra and a biting wind swept down off the distant mountains. It took an hour of steady slogging and no stops for rest to reach Hank and Emmitt's cabin. There was a light in the window and smoke whipped from the chimney.

We stopped in the brush a hundred feet from the cabin while Donovan studied it.

"Scuff your feet through the snow," Donovan whispered, "then your steps won't squeak. And remember, stay behind me and keep out of this."

We moved silently forward and stopped at the door. My heart was hammering so hard I was sure Hank and Emmitt could hear it. My knees had turned to water. This was no movie or something I'd read in a book. This was real! I knew I couldn't move fast if I had to. I thought I heard Hank's voice.

Then Donovan's driving shoulder hit the door, there was a splintering crash and he was inside. His rifle centered on Hank sitting on a bench beside the stove. He didn't see Emmitt, but I did. The open door partially hid Emmitt's bunk behind the door and Emmitt sat on the bunk.

Donovan was a step inside. Hank reared up from the bench and it went over with a crash. He reached for his pistol lying on the table. Then everything happened at once.

Emmitt launched himself from the bunk, landed on Donovan's back, pinned his arms, and tried to knock the rifle from his hands. The rifle discharged with an ear-splitting blast. The bullet slammed through the stove pipe and soot showered down. Hank let fly with a punch that caught Donovan on the side of the head. He dropped the rifle and the three of them collapsed in a wild tangle on the floor.

I stood frozen in the doorway. I'd seen fights in alleys, vacant lots. I'd been in two with Scrapiron. They were nothing. This was primitive savagery, death for at least one as they fought desperately for the rifle. There were shouts, grunts, curses, panting, and straining, the smash of heavy blows. Emmitt's pinning arms weren't going to let Donovan reach the rifle. That galvanized me. Without thinking, I jumped on Emmitt, twisted both hands in his long hair and began to yank. Emmitt's head bobbed back and forth, but he held on. I slammed my knee into the small of his back and he yelled. I gave him the knee again and again. He let go and I dragged him off backward.

Emmitt twisted, got to his feet, and hit me a wallop on the jaw that made me see stars. I shoved him away and cleared my vision. He charged back throwing wild punches. Instead of backing away, I stepped inside and caught him with a left hook that stopped him dead. Those colorless eyes blinked in surprise. A right slammed him against the wall.

I was on him crazy mad. Emmitt was as guilty of shooting Fawn as Hank, and maybe he had even done it. A couple of punches bounced his head against the logs. Then Emmitt set me back on my heels with a vicious one to the mouth. I tasted blood. Emmitt was about my height and twenty pounds heavier, but he was slow. I had to take advantage of that slowness.

I could hear Hank and Donovan fighting and I got a glimpse of Hank's face, twisted and bloody. Then I saw Donovan's and it, too, was bloody.

Emmitt knocked me flat, then aimed a kick at my face. I caught his foot, twisted, and brought him down. We thrashed around on the floor. Punches landed, punches missed. On the floor Emmitt used his superior weight. I slammed him under the chin with the top of my head and scrambled up. I kicked him in the stomach and he rolled to his back in agony. I dropped my full weight on him and he let out a yell.

Emmitt surged up and we stood toe to toe slugging wildly. Emmitt's punches shook me to my heels, but mine were getting through and driving him back. Suddenly Emmitt turned and dove for a rifle leaning against the wall. I tripped him, he fell, and I jumped over him and grabbed the rifle. He was getting up when I brought the barrel down on his head with savage force. Emmitt collapsed. He was out of the fight.

I whirled toward Hank and Donovan, boiling mad, ready to kill Hank. It wasn't necessary.

Donovan had Hank backed into a corner and Hank's coal black eyes were no longer sharp, probing, and mean. They were dull, his stare glassy. He was trying vainly to hold Donovan off, but Donovan was a raging demon. He slammed Hank's arms aside and waded into him. He was starting punches down around his knees and bringing them up with every ounce of strength in that tough, lean body. Every punch sounded like a butcher dropping half a beef on a butcher's block. Hank's arms were down, his head hung loose. He was helpless and Donovan was sinking him like a man driving a spike with a sledgehammer. Finally he collapsed on the floor. He was not out, but there was no strength left to rise. He fell over on his side.

The cabin was a wreck. Table was overturned, Stove knocked off its legs, flame and smoke belching from its open door. The bench was broken. Shelves were smashed and cans of food littered the floor. Only the lantern, hung from the ceiling by a rope, was not damaged.

Donovan pointed a finger at Hank and panted, "Come within a mile of my cabin and I'll kill you on sight." He picked up his rifle and said, "Let's go."

The fight still bubbled in me. "Just a minute." I gathered up both their rifles. Then I remembered something and began looking about. Against the wall on the floor, I found Hank's revolver. I put it in my pocket and, carrying both their rifles, I said, "Now I'm ready."

A half mile from the cabin I found a big rock. While Donovan watched silently I smashed the rifle stocks over the rock, then tossed them away. I took the revolver from my pocket, held it in my palm and said, "Hank said he'd carried this every day since he was fifteen — he'd feel naked without it." Then I beat it on the rock until the handle broke and the barrel split off. I threw them as far as I could in different directions. "Maybe he'll like walking naked through an Alaskan winter," I said and started off again.

It took hours to reach the cabin and I hurt every step of the way. Emmitt had given me a good beating, but I'd won. I kept thinking about that and in spite of the aches I felt wonderful. Neither of us spoke and I began thinking about Fawn. I wondered if she still lived.

At the cabin, before attending to our own wounds, we both knelt beside her. She looked dead. I put a hand on her chest and felt it lift slightly. I said, "She's still alive." At the sound of my voice she opened her eyes. Donovan said, "We've got to get liquid into her — she'll become dehydrated, then she will die."

He held her up, pried her jaws open, and I tried to pour a spoonful of water down her throat. She didn't swallow and it ran out. We tried several times more with the same results. Then I put the spoon further down, emptied it, held her jaws closed, and massaged her throat with a downward stroke. The third time she swallowed. We got half a cup of water down her before she quit.

"That ought to hold her for a while," Donovan said. He laid her down and asked, "You hungry?"

I shook my head.

"Me either. But we'd better wash up. Your face is something of a mess."

I looked at Donovan. One eye was getting black and was half closed. He had a long scratch on one cheek, a cut on the other. His mouth was puffed out of shape and his right cheek was swollen like a small balloon. I said, "You don't look so good yourself."

"Guess we're not what you'd call glamour boys." Donovan touched his cheek and winced. "That Hank packs a mean wallop."

"So do you. Hank was flat on his back when we left."

"I was lucky. The boxing I did in college came in mighty handy."

I remembered how he'd waded into Hank. "I'll bet you were good."

"Collegiate champ my senior year."

"You mean I've been living with a champion all these weeks?"

"I was no champion tonight. I got a couple of looks at you and I'd say you were doing a bang-up job on Emmitt."

I still had that warm, satisfied feeling. "That's the first real fight I've ever had. That left hook I hit him with at the beginning is the same punch I landed on Scrapiron. I'll bet if I'd followed that up as I did with Emmitt I'd have put him down. I might even have won. If I had," I added thoughtfully, "I wouldn't have been afraid to face Dad that night. I wouldn't have run away, watched my friend die, been in a snowmobile wreck, and wound up here in the wilds of Alaska. I wouldn't be fighting gangsters of some kind who steal trappers' furs and probably kill for them. And I wouldn't be nursing a dying wolf. Wonder what Dad would have thought if he'd seen this fight?"

"He'd have been proud as the devil. You were quite a tiger. There's a big chunk of man in there," he said, and tapped my chest. "If I didn't thank you before for going along, I do now. If you hadn't taken care of Emmitt they might have killed me. In fact, they probably would have. I didn't see Emmitt behind the door. All I had eyes for was Hank. They had me dead to rights. There's no doubt you saved me."

"Tonight should have told them something," I said. "Now maybe they'll lay off us."

Donovan shook his head, "I'd like to think so. But I doubt it. Hank and Emmitt don't know any other way. It's their life — the way they've always lived. It always will be."

"Then what will you do?"

"Been thinking about that. According to what you heard them tell the pilot, they plan to leave sometime this coming summer. It won't be too safe for them here after that. So until then I'll just have to be as careful as possible."

"They'll lay for you," I pointed out. "Like Hank said, they can be anywhere."

"I know. But I can't go to the police station and ask for protection or call the cop on the corner, or phone somebody. This is up here. Technically it's a state, but it's still more than half a million square miles of the last frontier in North America. There's a saying amongst old timers about this country: 'Up here you can get away with anything you're man enough to do.' It's just about right. As I told you before, and as all three of us know, nobody cares what happens to us. If we kill each other, we save the law a lot of trouble."

"There's got to be some way to stop them or get away from them. Maybe you could go to another cabin somewhere."

"They could follow. Even so, I don't know of another cabin around here where they wouldn't find us. You could spend months looking and not find one, especially in winter. No, this's the place to stay. I know the country better than they do. I can keep track of them here and I couldn't somewhere else.

"But something did change tonight. Your backing me in the fight the way you did. Your knowing about them, where they are and what they are, puts you in jeopardy, too. Even more than before. If you get out you can tell the authorities. After this fight, if there was ever any doubt in their minds, it's gone. They're sure you'll report them. For their own safety they can't let you leave. That puts you in this trap with me."

He smiled slightly, remembering. "You smashed their rifles and Hank's pistol. They can't do anything to us until they get new ones. For the present we've got them out-gunned. I wish we'd taken the short wave away from them. Now they'll have new guns in a week or two, as soon as they can contact that chopper pilot and have him bring them in. So we've got ten days to two weeks head start."

"Head start for what?" I asked.

He drew a deep breath, looking at me, "If you want to go out, hike out that two hundred miles.... I'll take you. Tonight you showed you're man enough to make it. It won't be easy, but I'm sure you can do it. It's the only way I know to get you out of this jam I'm caught in. How about it? You want to try? It's your decision."

Here it was! My way out! And it was handed to me by the one person in the world I'd never have expected it of. I just sat and looked at Donovan, believing and afraid to believe.

Somewhere I had read, or was told, that on rare occasions it is sometimes given to a person to look back and point to a certain time or incident and say, "That is where my life took a sudden turn." It can be good. It can be bad. It can bring you success or failure, make you a better person or a worse one. But it has affected your whole life.

This, I felt, was such a moment. Maybe the fight had something to do with it. I had taken on a very tough crook, possibly a killer, and beat him. Gone forever, I suddenly realized, was the boy who was afraid to face his father's wrath over a mere schoolboy squabble. A boy who kowtowed to a brother because he was a little older, bigger, and played football.

I thought of going home, of Dad and Rocky and the big house I'd lived in my whole life. Mother had died in her upstairs bedroom. I remembered the plaque hanging on the bedroom wall, "IT TAKES A HEAP OF LIVING TO MAKE A HOUSE A HOME." A heap of living had taken place in that house. The magnetic pull to return was stronger than anything I'd ever known.

But a heap of living had taken place up here on this wild tundra and in this lonely, isolated cabin, too. I looked at Fawn, a wild wolf, the only animal I'd ever had any close association with. I'd played with her, chased her, and she had chased me. I'd talked to her for hours and she'd answered with that breathy little bark, the tilt of her head and flick of her delicate ears. She had broken the dead monotony of dreary, ice-cold days. I awaited her appearance each day and missed her each day when she and Blackie left. In an odd way she saved my sanity. And now, largely because of me, she lay near death. I loved her and meant to do everything possible to save her.

I asked Donovan, "If we leave tomorrow or the next day, what happens to her?"

"I'm no vet," he said, "but even I can tell she hasn't much chance. Frankly, she may be gone by morning, almost for sure the next day or so. Don't let her influence you."

"She's not dead yet."

"No. Not yet."

I thought of the two hundred miles we'd have to travel in the dead of winter. The bitter cold that had no end. Most certainly we'd be caught in at least one raging blizzard. Somewhere along those bitterly cold miles it would be easy to come up with some kind of disabling injury. Even a turned ankle or fall could cause death.

Last, I thought of this man, Mike Donovan, lean, tough, sitting on the edge of the table, brown eyes watching me. Waiting on my decision. A decent man trapped in a web of circumstances and forced to live out his life up here in a small cabin in this frigid, unfriendly world. Once again he was caught in a trap from which there seemed no escape. He had saved my life. Now his was threatened. Donovan might have run once, but he was not the type to run again. And there was no place to run to. He was a lonely wolf with his back to the wall and he would fight to his last breath to live.

Someday soon there would be the inevitable showdown with Hank and Emmitt, the professional gangsters, the killers.

Donovan was not a killer, but he would have to become one to live here. And he was going to face those two alone.

I knew that if I stayed I'd be in this trap with Donovan. I owed this big man my life — and more. I'd been able to help him tonight. Maybe I could again. I couldn't let him face those two alone. I weighed all this against my desire to return home, the risks of trying to hike out, the danger I'd be facing every day and night with Hank and Emmitt on the prowl and trigger happy. And Fawn was lying at my feet barely alive. I made my decision.

"Mr. Donovan," I said, "if you can put up with me, I'd like to stay until the pilot comes in the spring."

"You know what you're up against, the risks you're running." He was watching my face closely. "We could have another set-to like tonight — or even worse."

"I know," I said.

Donovan rubbed a big hand across his bruised face. "I shouldn't let you stay, and I wouldn't if I knew a reasonably safe way to get you out." He was quiet a moment, his brown eyes studying me. Then he said softly, "Joel, you're quite a man. Yes sir, quite a man. That ruckus tonight really hardened and tempered the metal."

"The name's Joe," I said. "I don't like Joel much. My dad never understood that. He always called me Joel — or even 'Little' Joel."

He nodded, "Of course. 'Little' Joel is a boy's name. Joe it is. Mine's Mike." We shook hands gravely. Then he smiled. It was the first real uninhibited, open smile I had ever seen. On that rugged face with its cuts and bruises, scratches and swelling from the fight, it was as beautiful as sunlight breaking through storm clouds. That moment I loved Mike Donovan. Not as I loved my father, or Rocky, or Ross Edwards, or even my mother — but as one with whom I had shared the greatest danger two men can face together. Life and death. That moment my life changed. I knew it would never be the same again.

- 9 -

Now that I'd made the decision to stay, take care of Fawn and help Mike fight Hank and Emmitt if necessary, I felt surprisingly good. I told him so. "I don't understand it," I said. "For weeks all I thought of was going home, getting away from here. If anybody had told me anything could be more important, I wouldn't have believed them. Now I think being gone a few months is a good thing for both Dad and me. Turning your thinking around like this so fast doesn't make much sense, does it?"

"Makes a lot. You've found something that's more impor-tant to you," Mike said. "Now you know where you're going, what you're going to do. You've made a big decision, probably the biggest one in your life so far."

"Mother always made the decisions for me before. This past year Dad has."

"You're due to start making some of your own. You've grown up a lot since you've been here. I've seen it coming. You thought I neglected you — and I did. Deliberately. You were a kid. You had to grow up, toughen up, to live here even one winter. I figured the chances were at least ten to one nobody'd find you. So I let you go, but I watched you closer than you thought. Tonight you grew up."

"You were a tough teacher."

"Tough country takes a tough teacher."

"I know that now," I said. "Thanks." I sat down beside Fawn, touched the silken fur on her shoulder and spoke softly to her. Her eyelids twitched, but she didn't open them. Her ears moved at the sound of my voice. I said, "Should we try to give her more water?"

Mike bent forward and studied her. "She seems to be resting. Maybe we'd better let well enough alone for the moment. We'll try again in a couple of hours."

Mike touched his face gingerly, "I'm gonna wash up. My face hurts." I watched as he got out a pan, filled it with warm water, and went to work on his cuts and bruises with a rag and small hand mirror. When he finally finished he asked, "I look any better?"

"Yeah, a little. But you're gonna have a beaut' of a black eye and eating won't be any picnic for a couple of days."

"I know," he agreed. "You'd better try some soap and water on your face, too. It sure can use it."

I went through the same ritual. My cuts and bruises stung, and afterward Mike pronounced me moderately good looking. "Not exactly handsome, you understand, but you'll pass if the light's not too strong." He grinned at me, "Been quite a night and that's a fact. Think I'll turn in. You might as well, too. There's nothing we can do for Fawn until we give her more water."

"Think I'll just sit here," I said.

"Sure." Mike rolled over on his bunk. "Mind turning the light down a little? Wake me in a couple of hours, or if she shows any change."

I turned the light low, put a couple of sticks in the stove, and sat down beside Fawn again. I put a hand on her shoulder and stroked her lightly to let her know I was there and she was not alone. I felt her nose. It was hot. In dogs this was a bad sign. I could feel her breathing beneath my hand. But she did not open her eyes.

Sometime later I heard howling in front of the cabin and peeked out the door. Blackie sat where the two of them always waited for their meat. His nose was pointed at the stars. I had never heard such grief in an animal's voice. There was loneliness, sadness — an animal kind of heartbreak. It was as if he knew she was dead. That sound, riding the frigid Arctic stillness, made me sad, too.

Blackie kept it up for some time and finally Mike muttered, "Wish he'd quit. He knows."

Blackie's mournful howling finally ceased and once again silence, so complete and absolute I could almost hear it, closed in.

I replenished the stove, felt Fawn's hot nose and leaned back against the log wall and closed my eyes. The day's happenings had got to me. I was deadly tired. But I couldn't sleep. Every few minutes I roused, looked at Fawn and waited. Finally I woke Mike and we tried to get more water into her. Again I had to work the spoon deeper into her throat and then massage it before she swallowed. We got another half cup into her before she quit on us.

Mike turned in again. "You might as well get a little sleep. If she's still alive in the morning we'll do what we can for her. If she isn't, our troubles are over."

"I'll wait," I said.

"Sure." He rolled over and went to sleep.

I tried to stay awake. I felt the biting cold creep through the logs and drive the temperature down. I thought of replenishing the fire, but somehow I never got around to it.

I awoke on my bunk tucked into the sleeping bag and first dawn lighting the window. Mike had the fire going and was sitting on the bench looking at Fawn. I started up guiltily and Mike said, "When I woke up you were sound asleep so I tucked you in. That's quite a job with a guy your size."

"I didn't know how tired I was." I looked at Fawn. She lay utterly still. Her coat looked rougher than it had last night and it seemed her sides were more sunken in. She seemed almost thin. I asked fearfully, "Is — is she still alive?"

"She's alive. I don't know why."

I got on my knees beside her, carefully put a hand on her shoulder, and spoke her name. Her eyes moved behind the closed lids, but she didn't open them.

Mike said, "Let's get more water into her, then we'll boil a piece of meat, make a broth, and try to get that down her. The broth will be a little nourishment. That and keeping her comfortable is all we can do. The rest is up to her and nature. She's got two big things going for her. She's a wild animal and she's a wolf. Whether that's enough I don't know."

She took another half cup of water. Then we boiled a piece of moose meat and made a thick broth. We got nowhere with it. "We've done all we can," Mike said. "Now I guess we just wait."

Later I went outside for an armload of wood. Blackie sat there waiting. The moment I appeared he rose and stood wagging his tail. He was a couple of hours early. I figured he had seen Fawn disappear into the cabin yesterday and his wolf mind told him she must still be there.

I carried in the wood, then returned to the freeze room for a chuck of meat for Blackie. I dropped it in the snow as close as he'd permit me to approach and said, "She's hurt. You know that. We're trying to make her well again. You've got to be a good wolf and wait. You've got to be patient. I'll bring her back to you just as soon as I can."

Blackie cocked his head one way, then the other. His sharp ears jumped back and forth catching every change in my voice. He dropped his head almost to the snow and stared straight at me as he always did. But he didn't come forward until I backed away. Then he advanced to the meat, smelled it, and stood studying me. He seemed worried, uncertain, troubled. Something had happened to his mate. He was trying to understand. I guessed his mind was telling him that when he again saw her it would be here where she had disappeared.

Wolves mated for life. I guessed there was no bigger, stronger, more fearless wolf than Blackie in all the North. In a human he'd be called a bruiser — like my father and Rocky. One way or another, he could conquer anything in his world and he knew it. Now he had come up against something he could not handle, loss, grief, and death. He was groping, trying to understand what had happened to his world and to her.

It seemed I was always running into similarities. Here was another. I remembered what Ross Edwards, the pilot, had said about my father trying to find himself, keep his family together, and straighten out his life after Mother's death. I looked at this big, powerful wolf who was so perplexed, uncertain, and I said, surprised, "Why, you're a lot like my dad. He's a big, tough guy and he's been trying to adjust to Mother's death for a whole year. He's having rough going, too. And you're having it very tough. It's in your face. We're doing the best we can for Fawn. You can count on it. I just wish there was some way I could make you understand."

Blackie watched me until I turned back to the cabin. Then he picked up the meat and left. He did not trot away, head high, tail waving. He walked head and tail down, dejected, miserable, alone.

I watched him disappear and let this new thought unwind. I'd been so wrapped up in my own grief at losing Mother I hadn't been aware that Dad had been groping blindly through his own traumatic upheaval. I had always looked upon him as big, tough, indestructible. A juggernaut who plowed straight ahead scattering opposition and obstacles. A cool, efficient, emotionless machine. I knew now that wasn't true. It had taken a big, tough Arctic wolf to bring it home to me.

When I entered the cabin I told Mike about Blackie and my dad. "If I hadn't come north, I'd probably never have been aware of Dad's problems."

"You get down to basics pretty fast up here." He got into his parka and picked up his rifle, "Think I'll take a little hike. Want to stretch your legs?"

"Where do you go every day?"

"No place special. Just wander around, look at the tundra, the game. It's something to do and keeps me from thinking too much. There's nothing you can do for Fawn right now."

"I think I'll stay anyway. Don't forget Hank and Emmitt may be out there somewhere."

He smiled at that. "You smashed their rifles and Hank's revolver, remember? We're safe for a few days."

Today Mike Donovan was a different man. He smiled. He seemed cheerful. The drawn, tense look was gone from his face. There was warmth in his voice, a great sympathy in his brown eyes when he looked at Fawn, and he handled her tenderly, carefully. "I'll be back in a couple of hours," he said, "in time for her next watering and feeding."

Alone, I studied Fawn critically. She hadn't opened her eyes since last night. She hadn't moved an inch. Her flanks seemed more sunken this morning. Her nose was hot and dry. The only sign of life was the jerky rise and fall of her chest. One single bullet weighing little more than a nickel had done this. She needed more than water. She needed nourishment. All we had was moose meat and moose broth and she couldn't or wouldn't swallow the broth.

Then I had an idea. I heated the broth again, sat beside her, dipped a finger in the broth, pried her mouth open and put my finger inside. She closed her mouth and for a minute my finger just lay there. Then I felt her tongue touch my finger. She licked the broth off. I stroked her throat and she swallowed. I repeated it again and again. She got only a few drops. Maybe a spoonful was more than she could handle. I got the spoon, lifted her head to my knee, pried her jaws open and with the spoon half full emptied it into her throat. There was not enough to run out. I closed her jaws, held them shut, and stroked her throat. Finally she swallowed.

I talked to her, coaxed, and continued to feed her. She took a dozen of the half spoons, then quit.

When Mike returned I told him.

"That's fine, fine," he said. "Now let's get more water into her."

She took both water and broth, but I had to stroke her throat at each swallow. When we finished, Mike sat back on his heels and studied her.

"Is she going to make it?" I asked anxiously.

"I don't know. I can't say she looks better. Her nose is still hot and dry. Her whole appearance is rougher. It seems to me if she were going to make it, she should have shown some improvement by now. She hasn't. If anything, she's gone down a bit more. Has she opened her eyes?"

"No."

"Last night she did. She's so near gone she can't even do that." Mike rubbed a big hand across his face. "I hate to say this, but I've got a feeling she won't be here in the morning. I figure she'll go sometime during the night. We've no way of knowing what that bullet did to her inside. She could be bleeding internally, draining what little spark she has left."

"She's still breathing and swallowing," I pointed out. "I'm going to keep trying until — until she's gone."

Mike patted my shoulder, "Good boy. I'm with you all the way. Like I said, she and Blackie have been the only friends I've had."

We got supper and I noticed how the rich odors of cooking made Fawn's nostrils twitch slightly. But she didn't open her eyes or move.

After supper we got more water and broth into her. Mike said, "She should have a little solid food. Maybe if we cut some meat into very small pieces she'd swallow it."

I got a piece and diced it as small as corn kernels. We pried her mouth open and put two on her tongue. She wouldn't swallow them. We took them out.

Again we sat, watched, and waited. I sat cross-legged on the floor, Mike on the end of the bench. We'd been there some time when Blackie's mournful howling filled the night and brought a lump into my throat.

"Poor devil," Mike said. "He knows there's something wrong and there's no way to explain it to him. I wish he'd quit."

"I'm going to give him another piece of meat," I said. "He's not doing much hunting. He spends so much time here in front of the cabin he must be hungry."

I went to the freeze room and got a liberal chunk. Blackie was standing when I returned, a dark silhouette against the white snow.

I walked toward him and got closer than ever before he began backing away. I dropped the meat and said, "I'm glad you're concerned. We're doing all we can for her. I know it isn't easy, but you've got to be patient."

Blackie didn't pick up the meat until I reached the cabin door. I had the odd feeling that in some strange way he understood. But I didn't tell Mike. It would have sounded silly and childish.

That night we took turns watching over Fawn. I took the first two-hour watch. Then Mike took over.

Each time we changed shift we studied her and gave her all the broth and water she would take. I was on shift when Blackie began his mournful howling again. Sometime later, after Blackie quit, I again heard wolf voices. This time there were many. They were singing.

The sound began almost as a whisper and rose as more voices joined in until it was a complete chorus. They sang for the sheer joy of making music. Some voices were high, some deep. I identified individuals as the sound swelled and filled the deathly still Arctic night. The chorus died away, then began again and rose high and clear, filling all space. It went on and on and I forgot to wake Mike until it was over. Then we fed Fawn again. Finally I rolled into my bunk, but I couldn't sleep. I kept thinking of the wolves singing and wondered if it was some kind of dirge and they knew she was dying. I'd heard animals sometimes knew these things.

When Mike woke me it was morning and the first thing I asked was, "Is she still alive?"

"Still alive. Don't ask me why. Like I said, wolves are mighty tough animals."

We looked at her together and I, too, wondered why she still lived. Her flanks were definitely sunken. Her coat had further lost its luster. The hair was dull and grey and no longer had that well-groomed look.

Mike asked, "How's she seem to you?"

I shook my head. "No better, that's sure."

"What I figured." He felt her nose. "At least it isn't hot and dry if that means anything at this stage."

We gave her water again, almost a cup this time, and a like amount of broth. I stroked her throat to get her started swallowing. Then she did it on her own. But she'd done that before.

We made breakfast — bacon and sourdough pancakes. The cabin filled with the mouth-watering aroma.

I poured syrup over a pancake and was beginning to eat it when I glanced down at Fawn. Her big golden eyes were open, watching me, and her black nose twitched as she sucked in the delicious odors.

"Mike!" I said excitedly, "Look! Look!" I dropped my fork and was down on my knees. Mike knelt beside me.

Fawn's eyes were clear and intelligent, as if she were trying to place the enticing smells her sensitive nose was picking up.

"Son of a gun!" Mike said. "I'll be a son of a gun!" He reached up to the table, broke off a tiny corner of pancake, doused it with syrup, pried open her jaws, and put it on her tongue. For a few seconds it just lay there. Then her jaws closed, she chewed, and swallowed.

Mike tore off another and another and she ate them. Finally she refused to eat more. Mike sat back on his heels smiling. "That was something."

"She's going to make it! She ate, Mike! She ate!" I was so excited I stammered.

"It looks promising. But she doesn't look good." He began to frown.

"What's wrong?" I asked. "What's bothering you?"

"When I was a kid," he said thoughtfully, "I had an aunt who'd been sick a long time. One morning she woke up cheerful and bright and wanted a big breakfast. We all figured that was the turning point and she'd recover. A few hours later she died. Somebody, a doctor I think, said it was nature making a last valiant stand to throw off the disease. Whether it's true or not I don't know. I do know she died. I hope it's not the same with Fawn."

I patted her between the eyes and said, "I won't give up."

"If you won't, I won't. Let's try the broth again." She refused the broth.

We watched her for hours but she made no effort to move. She lay there and her yellow eyes followed me. We got all the liquid down her we could, and now I no longer stroked her throat.

She ate more pancake and we tried her on a small piece of meat. She ate it. By noon we could see she was improving.

I said happily, "She won't be like your aunt. She's going to make it…."

Mike nodded, "I think you're right."

Late in the afternoon Blackie appeared. I fed him and told him Fawn was going to be fine. Again I felt that somehow the big wolf understood.

That night Fawn lapped broth and water from a bowl. I tried to feed her pieces of meat but she refused.

Mike said, "Put it on the floor. She's a wild animal. She's not used to being hand fed."

She ate it off the floor.

I thought she might try to stand but she didn't. I spoke to Mike about it.

"She'll know when she can. Let her alone."

We extended our night watch to four hours so we each got a little more undisturbed rest.

Blackie put in his mournful session howling. Again it brought a lump to my throat. I decided that if she didn't walk by morning I'd carry her out so Blackie could see she was still alive.

After breakfast she had still made no effort to move. Blackie arrived an hour later and I said to Mike, "I'm going to take her outside so he can see she's still alive, then I'll bring her back inside. He's been very faithful. He's got a right to know."

Mike nodded, "We'll use the slab of broken sled. It's out in back. Carrying her might break something inside and we don't want to do that at this stage."

"You think I'm silly?"

"Not at all. I've read that some scientists say wolves have the intelligence of a seven-year-old child. If that's true, then Blackie knows what's going on. I was smiling to think how much you've changed since that morning I first found you. Then you wanted me to kill them both. I'll get the slab."

We eased her onto the slab and she only whimpered a couple of times.

Mike said, "Another reason I'm in favor, maybe when she sees him she'll make an effort to get up. She has to do that eventually to get well and strong. She's got to walk soon."

I pulled the piece of sled to the spot where the wolves always sat, dropped the rope, and said to Blackie, "There she is. You've been howling your head off every night for her. Come see her." I walked back to the cabin.

We watched from the doorway. Blackie approached a slow step at a time. Fawn lifted her head to him but didn't try to rise. Blackie stood there, tail waving, and licked her face. He walked around her barking low and urgent. The bark saying plainly, "Get up. Get up." But she didn't move. He reached out a paw and touched her muzzle. Then he lay down close beside her and put his big head across her back as if he were warming and protecting her.

For some minutes neither moved. Then Mike said, "We'd better bring her in. She's not going to get up. You want me to get her? Blackie might put up a protective row."

I shook my head. "Blackie knows me."

I walked forward slowly. Blackie rose and stood looking at me. He dropped his head in that peculiar 'about to charge' manner. Then when I was close, he began backing away. He stopped about twenty feet off, watched me gather up the rope and put it over my shoulder. He seemed uncertain what to do. I said, "Now you know she's alive. I'll bring her back when she can walk." He watched me all the way to the door.

We returned to feeding her every two hours. Early in the afternoon Mike went for a short walk. He fed Blackie as he left.

I watched Fawn. When her eyes were open she watched me. But she slept a lot.

The first thing Mike said when he returned was, "She tried to get up yet?"

"No. Maybe she's afraid to try, or is too weak."

"Could be. But being a wolf it seems she'd at least try."

Daylight passed into darkness. We lit the lamp. I talked to Fawn, coaxing her to try to stand. It was no use.

We'd eaten and fed Fawn, and Mike said suddenly, "Let's try something."

"What?"

"Maybe she needs to know she can stand and walk and run again. I was on crutches about four months. When the doctor took them away and said to walk I was afraid to try. Maybe she is, too. She's got to walk again or we'll have to destroy her."

"All right, what do we do?"

"I'll lift her to her feet. You stand off a little ways with a piece of meat and try to coax her to you."

I got the meat and squatted near the door.

Mike lifted her and set her on her feet. I called her and held out the slab of meat. "Come on. Come get it," I coaxed. "It's all yours." I held it toward her. Her sharp ears shot forward, her golden eyes centered on the meat. She licked her lips. Mike took his supporting hands away. Immediately her ears went back tight to her head, her head dropped. She lay down immediately. No amount of coaxing helped. She lay panting from that small exertion.

Mike shook his head, "Wish I knew what damage that bullet did inside."

"Maybe she needs more time," I said hopefully.

"We'll give her all she needs. But there's a point where no amount of days or hours will help. We can't be far from that time."

Mike didn't think it necessary to sit up with her. "I'll wake up a couple of times and check to see how she's doing."

I said, "I'll stay up with her for a while. I'll wake you if anything happens."

It was hours later. I had turned down the light, the cabin was cool but not yet cold. Blackie had put in his session of howling. A pair of wolves far across the tundra had sung a duet. I was leaning against the log wall, eyes closed, feeling discouraged when I heard the sound. I must have been half asleep because I heard it at least a minute before it registered on my sleep-drugged mind. Then I opened my eyes. The first thing I saw in the dim light was the shape of a wolf standing in front of me. I reached for the flashlight beside me, flooded the room and yelled, "Mike! Mike!"

Mike reared up on the bunk. Then he saw Fawn standing, head down, ears flattened, bushy tail tucked tight. But standing! He scrambled off the bunk and we both fell on our knees beside her. She looked at us with big yellow eyes, but she showed no pleasure at being up. She simply stood, trembling violently.

"She made it!" Mike said happily. "By golly, she made it! Go over by the door and call her. Take that chunk of meat with you."

I went to the door and called. She looked at me, then the meat. She licked her lips. Very deliberately she took a step, then another and another. She came to me slowly, painfully. But she came. She reached for the meat and ate it. Then I coaxed her back to Mike. There she collapsed on the skins and lay panting.

"When Blackie comes tomorrow we turn her loose with him."

"She's not strong enough," I protested.

"You'll be surprised how fast she'll gain strength now. Remember, she's not a domesticated dog. She's a wild wolf. As soon as she can get around at all she'll want out. She'll rip this cabin apart if we don't let her go."

I wasn't sure. But with morning I learned how right Mike was.

Blackie came early. How she knew he was out there I don't know. But she hobbled to the door and stood with her nose to the crack.

I opened the door. She walked out slowly, unsteadily. But there was eagerness in her waving tail, in her open mouth and lolling tongue. Blackie stood about fifty feet off. He would come no closer. She reached him. They rubbed noses a moment, then she lay down. Blackie licked her face and walked around her, tail waving.

I ran to the freeze room, got a chunk of meat, sliced it in two and took it to them. Fawn rose. They stood side by side and watched me approach. Blackie began backing away. Fawn stood her ground until I was five or six steps from her. Then she, too, began clumsily backing off. In the cabin I could pet and feed her.

The moment she was outside she realized she was free again. In that moment she became what her ancestors had been — a wild wolf.

I knew a moment of keen disappointment, then I realized this was how it had to be. I dropped the meat and backed away. Fawn limped forward and stopped at the meat. Blackie joined her. They stood there and looked at me. Across thirty feet of snow we studied each other and accepted each other for what we were — a human and two wild animals.

Then they picked up the meal and started away. Blackie broke trail. Fawn limped behind. After a couple of hundred feet she lay down to rest. Blackie waited patiently beside her. A minute later she rose. They went on single file and disappeared.

I returned to the cabin and asked Mike, "Do you suppose we'll ever see them again?"

"Why not? All we've done to them is be good. They know that. Don't worry, they'll be back tomorrow looking for their handout." He looked around, then smiled, "Seems a little empty in here. Think I'll take a hike out and see what's going on. Want to come?"

"Yes."

"Bring a rifle. It's time you learned how to handle one." He indicated the guns lined up along the wall. "Take that one. The three hundred. It's a lighter caliber, a good gun to learn on, and it packs plenty of hitting power."

We made a giant circle going further than I had ever gone alone. We raised plenty of game. A pair of moose crashed away. In the distance, a family of wolves moved through the brush and disappeared. An Arctic owl on a limb watched us pass. Ptarmigans exploded out of the snow almost under our feet. Rabbits were everywhere. A dozen caribou stampeded into the trees.

We stopped to rest at the edge of a brush patch and looked across the flat snow. Mike said, "This is what I've done almost every day the past three years. I doubt if there's a rock, tree or shrub in a radius of twenty miles I don't know personally. And I watch the animals and study them. I'd have gone crazy without this to occupy me. I've seen some donnybrooks of fights between a moose and a pair of wolves. A couple of grizzlies put on a real slugfest. You never know what you'll see." He was silent a moment, then pointed, "Like that for instance."

Perhaps a mile away, two figures trudged through the snow. Hank and Emmitt!

"I see they've got guns," Mike observed. "They got them mighty fast." They went up a low ridge and disappeared over the top. "The real predators," Mike scowled. "More cunning, more deadly, more vicious than wolves are believed to be. I wish now I'd made you leave the night we had the fight. We might have made it then. Now that they've got rifles again, it's too late."

- 10 -

Next morning Blackie and Fawn were back for their handouts of moose meat. They sat in front of the cabin and waited as if nothing had happened. Fawn's limp was hardly noticeable. After they left I mentioned this to Mike, "She hardly limps at all now and she didn't stop once to rest. How come so fast?"

"With a dog and a wolf, they're from the same family, their years run about seven to one compared to a human. A ten-year-old wolf would be about the same as a seventy-year-old person. One day for them equals about seven to us. So she recovered in one day what would take us a week."

With Fawn well, I could no longer approach Blackie any closer than before. He kept his distance, but to me it seemed he didn't look so worried. As for Fawn, once again five or six steps was as close as she would permit.

Now that I had made the decision to spend the rest of the winter in the North with Mike Donovan and we got along so well, returning home was no longer uppermost in my mind. But it was always there in my thoughts, a warm presence to think about when a sense of loneliness threatened to overwhelm me. For the most part, I discovered, there were any number of things to keep me occupied.

Every day after I'd fed the wolves and played a few minutes with Fawn, then watched them leave, we hiked out across the tundra. We ran Mike's trap line, which was short, and consisted of only a few traps because all he wanted was enough money to buy the things he really needed: shells, flour, sugar, coffee, food staples, and a few clothes. "What would I do with more money?" he explained. "And where'd I spend it and on what?"

After checking the trap line we hiked about the country. Fortunately, the cabin sat on a huge flat part of the tundra with few trees and only a little, low, scraggly kind of brush. "Out here," Mike explained, "we're reasonably safe from Hank and Emmitt. It would be almost impossible to ambush us in this open." But I noticed he was still careful and watched our back trail.

It was days before we glimpsed Hank and Emmitt again. They were trudging away in the distance across the ridge of a barren hill. To me they were no longer a threat to our safety. They were just a couple of men disappearing over the horizon. I said as much to Mike.

"Don't kid yourself." Mike's voice was tough, his face had that ugly look. "That's what they want us to think. But Hank's the main one. Never forget that. He's tough and cold-blooded. He has to be if he's killing trappers for their fur."

"If they want to kill us why don't they hide in the brush or behind a rock and take us as we pass?"

"You see much brush around here for them to hide in or big rocks to hide behind? We're out in the open for the most part and they'd leave tracks that'd tell us just where they are.

"And you have to remember," he continued, "the kind of men they are. They're used to doing their killing close up. They're not rifle marksmen. They're like most crooks, they want to be right on top of the victim. I doubt either of them ever had a rifle in his hands until they came up here. And at their ages you don't become an expert.

"If you'll check our backtracks," Mike continued, "you'll see we stay well out in the open. No place for them to hide, and fresh tracks across this snow would be a dead giveaway to their locations. They definitely don't want to run into us with our more powerful guns.

"I'm a good shot. I intend to make you one. I'm hoping we make it through without a shootout until the plane comes for you in the spring. There's only a couple of months of winter left, then you'll leave."

"You'll still be here," I pointed out.

"They don't worry about me. They know I can't turn them in because I'm wanted, too. But you can with complete safety and they know it. You're the one in the big danger. You've got to remember that."

I knew Mike was right. But my own reasoning told me that even a couple of murdering crooks would think twice before tackling us. We could take care of ourselves. We had taught them a pretty good lesson that night in their cabin, but I'd do as Mike said and be careful.

The days were clear and biting cold. The tundra was crisscrossed with whole networks of animal tracks and many had a story to tell. "Study them," Mike said. "All these things can help you to survive up here." In one place a pair of wolf tracks ran beside those of a floundering caribou. Coyote and fox tracks followed those of rabbits, their favorite food. Here a martin had caught an unsuspecting ptarmigan. A scattering of feathers told the story. A moose had backed against a cutbank where he put up a valiant but losing battle against at least a half dozen wolves. The snow was trampled. The struggle had been brutal.

Mike said, "Even a half dozen wolves manage to bring down their quarry in only about one of twelve or thirteen attacks on a grown moose. He's a terrific fighter. One swipe of his hoof can split a wolf's skull. The wolf is a very necessary animal. Most of his kills are of the old, the feeble, the sick. He keeps the herds healthy."

Each day I carried the three-hundred rifle. It was not as big or powerful as Mike's, but it would bring down any animal in the North if it was hit right. "Your job," Mike pointed out, "is to become a good shot."

So I filled my pockets with shells and practiced each time we went out — and we went almost every day.

At first I shot at small limbs on trees. Mike taught me to bring the gun up fast, center the cross hairs on the target, then squeeze off the shot. I shot at cans on stumps, cans tossed in the air. I learned to gauge the can's falling speed, to lead it, finally to drive it sideways.

"One of these days," Mike smiled after a particularly good day's practice, "I expect you to bring down a running rabbit, then to take off a ptarmigan's head."

"Why the head?"

"That's the smallest part and you don't damage the body meat."

That day finally arrived. I bagged several running rabbits, then we came on a flock of birds picking through the low brush. I chose a bird, came down fast, and squeezed the trigger. The ptarmigan's head disappeared and left the bird flopping in the snow. I got two more before they took flight. The last was a long shot for such small game.

Mike smiled proudly. "You've got a feel for the rifle. When you pull down on a ptarmigan he's as good as on the table. You're a marksman. I'd bet my life neither Hank or Emmitt could do that. We're gonna need another moose soon. You want to take him?"

"You think I can?" I was excited at the thought of shooting such a big animal.

"Why not," Mike smiled. "You just aim and the gun does the rest. But wait until we're close to the cabin so we won't have to carry the meat too far. And remember, the only reason we hunt is for the food. It's not a sport."

Again we saw Hank and Emmitt. Again they were disappearing over a distant ridge. Mike scowled, "I don't like it. They're shadowing us."

"Shadowing?" I asked.

"Following us. Sneaking around, keeping track of us, waiting."

"Waiting for what?"

"Some mistake we make that they can take advantage of."

"What sort of mistake?"

"Going into an area of high, thick brush, lots of trees. A nest of small canyons and ravines where it's easy to hide and they can be on us before we know it. It's a little like in the city. And being city men that's how they think. In the city if you don't want to take the chance of being mugged, stick to the main, lighted thoroughfares. Hit men are brave only when they have a definite advantage. That's what these two are looking for. In the meantime, Hank will worry us in a lot of little ways because that's how he is."

We were down to the last hundred pounds of moose meat when the blizzard hit.

It swept down off the distant mountain range, ripped across the flat tundra, and hurled its might against the cabin walls. We carried in loads of wood and kept the fire going. "This's a good time to get in a lot of sack time," Mike said. "Do like the animals, find a shelter somewhere and sleep it through."

"Will the wolves do that, too?" I asked.

"Nope. Blackie and Fawn'll be here same as usual for their handout."

And they were. I peeked out the door when I figured it was about time and there they were, patiently waiting while the howling wind combed their thick fur.

I got into my parka, ran to the cache, got two chunks of meat, fed them, and sprinted back to the cabin. Already I felt like I was freezing. This wind would cut through any parka made. Now I understood why Mike didn't want to hike me out to civilization. The fury of this storm scared me. I told Mike so.

"Good," Mike said. "Always remember panic can kill you as quick as the storm. Almost always you can figure something to do at such times. Just keep your wits about you and you'll make it."

The storm lasted three days. When we awoke the fourth morning it was deadly quiet. I opened the door and looked out at the white, quiet world. A drift had blown against the door three feet deep. I kicked it away and stepped outside. As far as I could see the world lay flat and glistening white.

Mike said, "This could be the last big storm of winter. From here on the weather could be pretty much down hill to spring."

I thought of something and asked, "How far off is spring?"

"Couple of months. Why?"

"You don't keep track of the days and months?"

"Why should I? When the snow starts to melt and the buds come out, I'll know it's spring."

"What month do you think this is?"

Mike thought, "Could be about the middle of March. Why?"

"If it is, I've got a birthday the fifteenth."

"No fooling? How old?"

"Eighteen."

"For a fact you're getting on. Your dad ever give you a birthday licking?"

"No. Why should he?"

"No kid should have a birthday without a licking."

"I've had eighteen without one."

"Seventeen." Mike made motions of rolling up his sleeves. "You're getting your eighteenth now. Your education's been sadly neglected." He made a grab for me.

I ducked and leaped outside into the snow where he couldn't corner me. Mike followed, grinning, reaching for me. "Come on, you might as well take your licking."

I crouched. "No way." I had watched wrestlers practicing at school. I remembered some of their tricks and holds that a friend on the team had shown me. Suddenly I dove at Mike's legs and knocked him flat in the snow.

Mike scrambled up wiping snow from his face, "Son of a gun, he means it!" He feinted at my legs, then grabbed my arm, yanked me around, tripped me, and fell on top of me.

But I rolled out from under him and with a quick turn was on top. I got a full nelson, but Mike broke the hold and tossed me over his head. Mike tried to pin me but again I slipped away. Mike was no wrestler. He tried to hold me with sheer strength. But I was never there. I tried every hold I knew but Mike broke them all. For several minutes we scrambled about searching for holds, breaking them, trying to get an advantage. First one, then the other was on top. We were yelling, laughing, panting, snow was flying. We finally wound up facing each other on hands and knees about three feet apart when we heard the low bark. There sat Fawn and Blackie watching us, ears snapping back and forth, heads tilting, curious. They'd come for their handout of moose meat.

Mike sat back on his heels, "Okay if we call this a draw?"

"Why not," I said.

We shook hands and scrambled up. Mike said, "You'd better feed 'em before they think we've gone completely crazy."

I ran and got meat and fed them. When I entered the cabin Mike was stripping off his clothes and shaking out the snow. "You better do the same," he said. "In the North you always keep dry. Your life can depend on it." He grinned and went on, "That was the most fun I've had in three years up here. You're a fast, slippery character. I really tried to pin you."

I said thoughtfully, "You're bigger, stronger, and twice as fast as Scrapiron. Bet I could take him now, or at least make it a real fight."

"You going to try him when you get home?"

I thought about it and shook my head. There'd be some satisfaction beating Scrapiron, but the reason still wasn't big enough. "Only if he wants it," I said. "Then I'll take him."

"You're really growing up," Mike smiled.

A couple of days later we jumped a young bull moose within half a mile of the cabin. Mike pointed, "There goes your moose. Take him. He ought to stop and begin to browse in the next quarter mile or so. That'll give you a chance to slip up within a hundred yards. Perfect range for the three-hundred."

"What'll you do?"

"I'll cut through this brush and make a big circle so he doesn't get my wind. He's heading for that little ravine up ahead. I'll come out at the top of the ravine after I hear you shoot."

I took out after my first big game. The moose was still trotting far ahead of me, doing exactly as Mike had said. For the first few hundred yards I followed in the moose's tracks. Then I took to the brush to get close. I was anxious, excited, a little apprehensive. A moose was no rabbit or ptarmigan. I hurried, trying to gauge the distance ahead. Twice I stepped into the open to look. The moose had slowed to a walk. Then he entered a small ravine and stopped to browse. I slipped into the brush to get closer.

The snow-laden brush was thick along the lip of the ravine and I lost sight of the moose. But I had his position well in mind. I crept silently forward taking advantage of every ground cover. When I judged I was within easy rifle range, I stepped carefully into the open.

There was no moose!

A couple of hundred yards away he was disappearing over the ridge traveling fast. There was no use following.

I was turning to go back when I caught a movement at the edge of the brush a hundred yards downhill. I thought it might be another moose and dropped flat in the snow behind a log and peered over the top.

Down there Hank and Emmitt stepped into view. They stood looking beyond me at the disappearing moose. I knew instantly they were not interested in the moose. They were looking for me. Suddenly raw fear was a hammer blow in the pit of my stomach. They'd been shadowing me all along. Now they had me separated from Mike. And at the moment I didn't know where Mike was.

- 11 -

Hank was doing the talking, gesturing, pointing. What he was planning — almost his words — was clear in his gestures, his looks, his sweeping arms. They knew I was somewhere close. Hank was laying a trap to kill me. Shock smashed through me and at the same time a cool part of my mind was not surprised. Mike had been trying to hammer this into me the past months. I remembered his words, "Hank's got to think you're the most dangerous man in the world to them. And he's right. You can turn them in and he knows you will."

I thought about that now as I watched Hank pantomime his plan to get rid of me. Once I was out of the way they could easily handle Mike, if they wanted to.

It seemed I was always facing some life-and-death decision. I couldn't let those two get at me or Mike. The final decision was mine. Then dread and fear was replaced with anger. There they stood not more than three hundred feet away, a pair of deadly dangerous jackals whose only excuse for living was to prey on decent people. At more than half this distance I had taken a ptarmigan's head off cleanly — not once but three times.

I could take Hank. Emmitt didn't matter. Without Hank, Emmitt was nothing. I didn't have a choice. I could end this fear, this daily sneaking around, this cat and mouse, life-and-death uncertainty here and now.

I eased the rifle over the log and centered the cross hairs on Hank's big head. I had him dead in the sights. My mouth was dry, my heart hammered so hard it shook the rifle muzzle. My eyes blurred. I stealthily raised a hand and rubbed them. I could wait no longer. Any moment those two would separate, disappear back into the brush in their search for me and I'd lose this chance. I had to do it now. Mike had been right all along. Those two, especially Hank, would never rest as long as one of us was alive.

Again I carefully slid the rifle barrel forward. I snuggled my cheek against the cold stock and brought my eye forward to the scope. Again Hank's head filled the scope with the cross hairs dead center. I had him! It was the easiest kind of shot. All I had to do was take up the trigger slack and our troubles would be over.

I could even see the expression on Hank's hawk-sharp face, his thin lips moved as he talked. I knew how those cold, black eyes were calculating, planning.

My finger took up the slack in the trigger. Practice had taught me at just the spot the rifle would fire. Another eighth of an inch. I could visualize what would happen. Hank's head would not disappear as the ptarmigan's had. It would be scattered all over the snow.

I began to shake. I couldn't get enough breath. I took a deep breath and slowly let it out. It did not help. I willed myself to pull the trigger, but I couldn't. I told myself that this very moment Hank was planning how to kill me. It didn't help.

I shifted the muzzle downward. Hank had the butt of his rifle in the snow and was holding it by the barrel while he talked to Emmitt.

I drew a bead on the rifle's magazine and squeezed the trigger. With the explosion, the rifle flew from Hank's hand and was hurled into the snow ten feet away. Hank let out a yell, grabbed his hand, and he and Emmitt dived back into the brush out of sight.

I jacked another shell into the barrel and waited. Then I heard the sounds of their crashing through the brush and saw the tops shake as they ran away.

I was still standing there trembling with reaction when Mike stepped into the clear several hundred feet above and came down to me. He saw the tracks of the moose going over the ridge and said in surprise, "You missed him! I don't believe it."

I shook my head. It was still hard to talk. "Not the moose. Hank and Emmitt."

"What!" Shock tightened his lips, the brown eyes, suddenly sharp, darted about. "My mistake." he said. "We separated. We shouldn't have. I didn't think they'd come this close to the cabin. What happened?"

I told him as we walked down to the spot where Hank and Emmitt had stood. Hank's rifle lay in the snow twisted and ruined. I was amazed at the power of the three-hundred. Mike picked it up, looked at it, and tossed it aside. "New," he said, "but once again not a powerful gun that will reach out the way ours will."

"I could have ended this whole suspenseful nightmare," I said. "I wanted to. I really tried. I had him dead to rights," I shook my head. "I couldn't do it. I just couldn't do it."

Mike smiled, "I know what you mean. I'm glad you didn't. The knowledge you've killed a man, even one like Hank or Emmitt, is a terrible burden to carry. I'll carry mine until the day I die. You handled it right."

"This brings them down to one rifle," I said hopefully. "That should help until they can get another, shouldn't it?"

"I doubt it. I'd guess that when they got more rifles this time they got extras — just in case. The one thing it has done, it'll make them more careful. That was a good shot you made on Hank's gun."

We headed back to the cabin. Neither of us felt like hunting any more that day.

At the cabin Mike was quiet. The morning's happenings seemed to have started a somber train of thought. For several hours he sat on the bench by the stove, kept the fire going, and stared thoughtfully at his big, clenched hands.

Blackie and Fawn came. I fed them. Fawn was frisky and wanted to play. I chased her, then she chased me. She didn't play long. Since the gunshot wound her play time seemed to have shortened.

I mentioned this to Mike when I returned inside. He acted like he hadn't heard. He said, "Sit down, Joe."

I sat on the bench on the opposite side of the table and waited. Finally he said, "This morning got me to thinking again. When you're trapped you keep looking for a way out even when you know there isn't one. You're like a caged lion that keeps pacing and pacing and looking and looking. I've been doing that for three years. Been thinking of something you said some time ago. It keeps sticking in my mind. This morning brought it back again."

"What was that?"

"You're pretty sharp and your dad's a sharp lawyer. I've heard of his firm and of him. You said you want to be a lawyer, and I gather you already know quite a bit about law. You said that in my case a good lawyer would figure out a defense. That there's extenuating circumstances, I think you called it."

"That's right."

"Name some."

"All right," I said. "You went to your partner's place for a legitimate showdown. You had discovered he was robbing the company. Can you prove that?"

"The books can."

"He pulled a gun on you. It was his gun, right?"

"Had to be. I don't own one. He took it out of a desk drawer."

"In the struggle it went off," I continued. "Dad would use that, and big. He'd show you how you'd been robbed over a period of time. It was his gun you were fighting over. That has to be self-defense. Dad would dig for other facts and he'd find them. I've known him to build a good case on less and win."

"What about my wife? Arlene was there. How much she saw I don't know. But she did see me standing with the gun in my hand and Frank dead at my feet. I knew she'd been slipping out to meet him. You said maybe she was trying to help me. That she knew what was going on. You believe that?"

"She could have known, couldn't she?"

Mike nodded, "I suppose so. She was the bookkeeper the first couple of years. She knew the business."

I tried to think as Dad would. "Let's assume she knew. This Frank was a good friend, your partner. Would she say to you, your friend is robbing you blind?"

"Of course not," Mike was emphatic, "not without a lot of proof. We'd been friends too long."

"There you are," I smiled. "She started seeing him, trying to draw him out, searching for facts. I don't know what she'd do or how she'd do it. But Dad would find something. You lived with her fifteen years. Don't you believe it could have been that way?"

Mike rubbed a big hand across his face. He clenched and unclenched his fists. His brown eyes had a far away look as if he were remembering things long past. Finally he said in the soberest voice, "It could have been. It could have been exactly as you say." He shook his head in wonderment, "Why didn't I think of that?"

"Did you talk to her after the fight or call her or get in touch in any way?"

"I just ran."

"You panicked."

"To put it mildly."

"That's good," I said.

"Good? What's good about it?"

"It's more proof you hadn't planned to kill him. Dad will play that up big. I don't think, with the right defense, you've got much to worry about."

"Which brings us to the crux of the problem," he said. "I've no money. If the company's operating I might get a little there. But I can't count on that."

"Dad will take your case for nothing."

"I don't take charity," Mike said stiffly. "I pay my way."

"You saved my life," I pointed out. "Put that into dollars and it's worth ten times more than any bill to defend you. He doesn't take charity either. You going to deny him the right to pay his debt to you?"

"It's different."

"A debt's a debt," I said.

"You'll make a good lawyer," Mike smiled.

"I hope so."

Mike sat scowling at his hands the longest time. When he finally looked up he was smiling. "Sure be great to go into my factory again, hear her humming, see people working. Wonder if they've made many changes?

"Things I want to say to Arlene, too. We were high school sweethearts. Soon as we got out of college we were married. It was tough going the first years. No kids. We should have had one, anyway.

"There's a big fancy restaurant up in the hills above the city. Always wanted to go there. Somehow we never made it. That's the first thing I'm going to do, take her to Hilltop. You're invited." His brown eyes were smiling in happy anticipation.

"Then it's settled?" I asked.

"Settled." We shook hands on it. Mike slapped the table. "I can hardly wait for spring and the pilot to come. Maybe there's still a life for me. I'm glad that if you had to get stranded and crash a snowmobile it was where I could find you. It's the greatest thing that ever happened to me. Now all we have to do the next few weeks is keep out of Hank and Emmitt's way and stay alive."

"There's something else," I said. "Since you're going back, it's time you started getting ready to enter civilization again. You've got a scissors here. It's time you got a haircut."

Mike touched the braids on either side of his head, "You're right, but the shop on the corner is closed for the day."

I got the scissors out of the drawer. "We're gonna open it," I said. "Turn around."

"You got a license to do this?"

"Not exactly," I clicked the scissors, "but I'm the best around. Come on, let's get started, I need the practice."

It was far from a professional job, but he did look more like a man who could appear in court when I finished than he had before. Mike ran his fingers through it and smiled at me, "Any time you want a recommendation I'll give you one."

- 12 -

We got our moose the next morning within three hundred yards of the cabin. I had fed the wolves, played with Fawn, and after they'd left we started out for a swing around the tundra. He walked into the open in front of us. Mike said in a quiet voice, "There he is! Take him, Joe! Take him!"

The moose collapsed at the shot. He was dead when we reached him.

It took most of the day to skin him out, carry in the meat, and hang it in the cache.

Fawn and Blackie came again as we were carrying in the last big pieces. They sat and watched. I cut two big chunks and took it out to them. "There you are," I said. "You can't get fresher meat in any market in the world."

Mike watched them trot away and observed, "They ought to be denning up soon."

"Why?"

"To have a family. It's getting that time of year. Maybe they've found a place close around here."

"You mean they dig a hole in the ground?"

"Or they might have found an old den some other family used in the past and moved in. They sometimes use the same den for years. I've a hunch it could be close. Keep an eye out for a hole in a cutbank. That's one of their favorite kinds of spots."

In the following weeks we never saw hide nor hair of Hank and Emmitt. Mike was sure they were watching, but were being especially careful not to be seen. It would have been easy for me to become complacent again and lulled into a false sense of security. But I remembered how Hank directed Emmitt to sneak on me that morning and I remained careful.

The days slipped away. Now that he had decided to go out with me and fight for his life, Mike became cheerful and open. He questioned me endlessly about Dad and different cases he knew of. I knew a little about many of them and explained how Dad had gone about their defenses.

Mike talked constantly about going outside. "Know how long three years up here can be?" he asked once. "An eternity. But even bad things can come to an end. I've got a theory. The good of life and the bad balance out. It's never all one or the other. Man couldn't stand it if it was all bad. You've got to have some bad to appreciate the good. I've had the bad. I can't wait for the good to begin. You're sure," he asked for the hundredth time, "your dad will take my case even though I've got no cash in hand to give him?"

"He'll take it. Stop worrying."

Mike nodded, smiling, "Getting worse than an old man. But if you knew how good it feels just to think of getting back."

"I've a pretty good idea."

"I guess you have. This has been a rough time for you. You're ready for some good things to happen, too."

"I'll take it like it comes."

Mike slapped me on the back. "Spoken like a man."

Mike laughed a lot these days. He talked a lot. It seemed to me he even looked younger. The deep lines in his cheeks and forehead seemed to be smoothing out. He was a different man from the one who'd found me in the wreck of the snowmobile.

The daylight hours lengthened. The sun began working higher in the sky. Gradually the thermometer began climbing. I felt the air turning soft, but it was still below freezing. Next, the animals that had spent the winter tunneling beneath the snow emerged to dart about searching for food.

"Spring's coming," Mike said happily. "It's about a month, maybe less, away. It'll hit with express-train speed. Up here it doesn't fool around about it. One week it's spring, the next summer. My last up here." He stretched his arms. "Man, I can hardly wait. I'll bet I've put my footprints on almost every square foot of tundra for twenty miles around."

"I haven't," I said. "It seems we go about the same places every day. Isn't there something else I should see before I leave?"

"Guess you're right. Hank and Emmitt have sort of restricted our travels." Mike scratched his head. "Plenty of things to see around here, but it takes time to get to 'em. There's the mine shaft the old prospector that lived in this cabin worked on for years. I told you he was a gold prospector. Not too sharp, I'm afraid. He always thought he was going to strike it rich. How many years he worked in that shaft I've no idea, but he dug a hole that runs back into the hills almost three hundred yards and he shored it up with timbers he cut himself. He did an amazing amount of work for one man."

"Did he strike gold?"

"Just enough to keep him working year after year. Every year when I came up to hunt it was always the same story: 'I haven't hit her yet. But I'm gettin' close.'"

"Where is the mine?" I asked.

"About a mile and a half from here."

"I'd like to see it. I've never seen a gold mine or any kind of mine."

"Just a tunnel into the side of a hill with an opening about six or seven feet square. Nothing much to see," he said.

"I'd still like to see it."

"We'll go tomorrow morning."

The mine didn't look like much. It did show a tremendous amount of work by one man. There were huge piles of earth that had been laboriously hauled out of the tunnel. The mine opening was a hole in a mountain of loose shale rock. An old iron wheelbarrow, several shovels, and a pick lay nearby. Apparently no one but Mike had been here since the old man had been found dead of a heart attack at the entrance.

"What will happen to it now?" I asked.

"Nothing," Mike said. "It's just a hole in the ground on federal land. Not worth a thing. Want to go in a ways? It's all shored up and safe."

"Yes."

Mike found a pitchy limb and slivered it with a shovel blade for a torch. He held it above his head and we entered the dark shaft. The air felt damp, but after a few feet it was warm and dry. The sides and ceiling were mixed dirt and rock held back by timbers. The floor was inch-deep in dust.

The ceiling lowered. Mike bent and held the torch down. I asked how the old prospector knew if he found gold in the dark.

"He brought the dirt out in a wheelbarrow and ran it through sluice boxes he'd put in the creek. The creek's only a few feet away. It's frozen solid and covered with snow now. In summer it runs."

"With all this work he never found his fortune?"

"Like I said, just enough to keep him excited and digging."

We went in about a hundred yards, then Mike stopped. "This is really all there is to see. It goes back another couple of hundred yards. Just a long tunnel into the hill. You seen enough?"

"Yes."

We were about half the distance back when a crashing wave of sound rolled down the tunnel and engulfed us with the smashing and banging of rocks, the rifle-sharp snapping of timbers. The distant dot of light that was the entrance was snuffed out. The smell of dust drifted down the tunnel to us.

Mike said, "What the devil! A cave-in. That doesn't make sense."

We hurried to the entrance. A huge pile of earth, rocks, sand, and gravel had spilled into the cave. The shoring timbers at the entrance were smashed. There was not even a sign of the opening left.

Mike climbed the slide and flashed the torch about. After a short inspection he came down. His face had the angry, ugly look I hadn't seen in weeks. Even his voice had an angry, grating sound. "This was no accident."

"What do you mean? Rock slides happen all the time."

"Not with this particular timing and in this particular way. This was triggered. All it took was a couple of iron pry bars. I saw some lying outside in the snow. Prying in just the right place against a big rock would set it off."

Mike's words were a cold wind blowing through me. I could hardly keep the quaver out of my voice. "Hank and Emmitt!"

"I knew they'd been shadowing us, just waiting," Mike said. "We played right into their hands when we came in here. There could be as much as a hundred tons of rock and gravel sealing this shaft. They've got us really stoppered. This is better than shooting us. No bodies to get rid of. We simply disappeared."

"It's my fault," I burst out. "If I hadn't wanted to see this — this hole in the ground — it'd never have happened."

"Maybe not, but something else would have. Don't blame yourself. I'm the one should have known better. I got careless. Hank counted on that. He knows human nature. He's sly, he's clever."

"What do we do now?"

"First, we've got to find some pitch sticks. This one will only last another half hour or so. There must be more lying around. It's the only light the old man had."

We found a half dozen wedged into cracks along the wall.

I asked, "Would it do any good to explore to the end of the tunnel?"

"I doubt it. The old man told me the tunnel goes straight back into the mountain. So the further we go the more rock and earth would be over us. Our only chance is to try to move these rocks and earth aside and dig our way out. And we don't have even a shovel. It's bare hands gopher digging."

"If we do get out Hank and Emmitt will likely be waiting for us."

"Maybe, but I doubt it. They'd have to sit out there hour after hour, maybe day after day, where it's cold waiting. I think they're so sure of us they feel perfectly safe leaving. Well, here's where we fool 'em." He skinned out of his parka, jammed the

114

torch into the crack of a rock and began rolling rocks away and digging with his bare hands.

I shed my parka and joined him.

We burned up three torches before we finally took a break and looked at what we'd accomplished. It wasn't much. My fingers were bleeding and raw, the nails cracked and torn. So were Mike's. We hadn't made much of a dent in the slide. We had three torches left. About another three hours light, then we'd be in total darkness.

Mike had been digging at the top of the slide. He'd push the rocks down and I shoved them on into the dark at the bottom of the slide. Mike had dug under and partially around a big rock that must have weighed hundreds of pounds. "Now this one," he said, "could be the key rock they broke loose that brought down the whole mass. If I can get this one out, I'd like to see what's behind it. So watch it, Joe. I'm going to dig more on this side. Keep clear when it breaks loose."

He began digging loose gravel from around the base of the rock. He worked down to another rock wedged beneath the big one. He worked at it, pushing gravel down to me. I shoved it further down out of the way. Finally Mike wiggled the underneath rock. He grinned at me. "Stand clear. When this big baby breaks loose it could do us a lot of good."

He pulled and levered at the underneath rock. It finally broke loose and came sliding down. The big one hung. Then it suddenly came. Instead of coming straight down, it twisted sideways and came bounding down the slope. I yelled, "Mike! Look out! Look out!" He scrambled out of its bounding path. I wouldn't have dreamed a rock that size could move with such lightness and speed.

Mike would have made it, but his feet slipped in the loose gravel and he sprawled flat. The big rock rolled over him. He let out a single piercing scream of agony. Then the rock was past. It came to rest on the floor a few feet from me.

I clawed my way up to Mike. He lay still and sprawled on his back. His eyes were open, staring at the ceiling. "Mike," I said, "Oh, Mike!" I was half crying. "Are you hurt? Are you hurt bad?"

Mike looked at me, his face blank with shock. There was blood on his lips. I wiped it away with my sleeve. Mike turned his head, spit a mouthful of blood, and looked at me. His voice was a shocked whisper, "That was an awful big rock. Awful big! I could feel things breaking inside."

"I'll get you down and we'll see."

"I can't move," he whispered. "I feel numb."

"I'll move you easy as I can." I got both hands under his arms and began easing him down the slide. "Tell me if it hurts too much." Mike didn't complain and I got him to the bottom and stretched him out on the floor. I bent over and asked, "Where do you feel numb? Where did the rock roll over you? Your legs?"

Mike shook his head. It was an effort to speak. "Legs are okay." He made a circle with one hand across his chest and stomach and down to his hips. "All here. It's beginning to hurt."

I looked up the slide. We'd been working more than two hours and I could scarcely see what we'd accomplished. Now I'd be working alone and it would go half as fast. Even if there was a way out it was going to be too slow. Mike was hurt bad. I had to get him out faster. I said, "I'm going to light another torch and explore further into the tunnel. I just might find a way out."

Mike nodded, "Sure."

With the second torch I probed deeper into the tunnel, well past the spot where we'd turned back. For a distance it was level, then I felt it tip downward. There was no use going further. I stood, trying to think. I reviewed the few options I had. Mike had said he could feel things breaking inside. I had to get him out fast somehow. I didn't like that spitting blood. My life and his depended on the next few hours. I had two possibilities, explore further and hope to find a way, or continue digging at the mountain of rubble blocking the entrance.

The tunnel was going deeper so further exploration was useless. That left the mountain of earth blocking the entrance. Dim as it was — maybe — just maybe — there might be a hole a couple of feet down just waiting for me to find it.

I returned to Mike, made him as comfortable as I could with his rolled up parka under his head and mine over his body, and said, "I'm going to dig more here."

He tried to smile, but it didn't come off.

I attacked the pile again with bare hands. It seemed I moved a lot of rock and dirt. I used up two torches and lit the last one. I had to stop to rest. My arms ached, my throat was bone dry. My hands and fingers were raw. Dust from digging stung my eyes and plugged my nostrils. When I glanced up to see what I'd done it was pitifully little. There was about an hour of burning left on the torch, then darkness.

I thought what this darkness would mean. In it was slow, agonizing, tortuous death. In this stygian tomb I could live days. With his injuries, Mike would not. Mike would be lucky.

Ahead were bone-dry, thirsty days and strength-sapping hunger. I'd become weaker until I could no longer even crawl. And always there'd be this utter dark and tomb-like silence. The moment this last torch sputtered out, the fate of both of us was sealed.

I wanted to scream, yell at the top of my lungs, but there was no one to hear. I wanted to fight something. And the only thing I could fight was this mountain of earth and rock that I'd been tearing at for hours with so little success. A wave of help-lessness engulfed me. I stood on the slide and hung onto my emotions with both hands to keep from flying apart.

- 13 -

Finally I got control of myself and went down off the slide to check on Mike. A movement at the dim edge of the torch light caught my eye. I looked again, squinting to be sure. I rubbed my eyes because this had to be a figment of my imagination, or a trick of my dust-burning eyes. Then she walked into the full light of the torch and stood looking at me. Her head was cocked, sharp ears forward, her tongue hung out in that wolfish grin I knew so well.

I called her name, "Fawn! Fawn!" I went stumbling off the rock pile.

She immediately backed away.

I dropped on my knees and held out my hand. "Fawn," I coaxed, "don't run away. Please don't run away. You know me. It's Joe, who feeds you and Blackie every day. Oh, Fawn, where did you come from? How did you get here? How? How?" In my excitement I began to stammer.

She backed off keeping those five paces between us.

Mike whispered, "What's up?"

"It's Fawn, she's in here. She's standing just a few feet from me. It's Fawn, Mike! Fawn! There's got to be an opening we missed somehow. Unless...." My heart dropped into my shoes, "unless she came into the mine entrance that's plugged now."

Mike's words were labored, spaced, "Not — likely. Wolves — don't — like big — openings — to — their dens. Just — enough to — crawl — through. We'd — have — seen — tracks — coming — in."

"Then there's got to be an opening somewhere. I'm going to leave you for a few minutes and see if she'll lead me out."

Mike moved a hand, "Luck."

I approached Fawn carrying the torch. I was very careful, slow. The torch worried her and she acted ready to run. If she took off I'd lose her in the dark. "Go ahead," I coaxed softly, "show me the way out. Show me how you got in. We saved your life once. Now you can pay us back."

She kept backing away as I approached. Her sharp ears twitched back and forth as if understanding my every word. Finally she turned and began picking her way over the floor, staying just at the edge of the torch light. I followed, letting her take her own time. When she stopped, I stopped. When she went on, I followed.

I felt the floor tip down again. Here I had turned back.

Fawn went on.

A dozen steps further the floor began to rise. We came to a huge stone that blocked half the tunnel. Beyond it more tunnel disappeared into the solid black. At the far side of the stone Fawn turned right into a small side passage.

This passage was narrow and low. I had to follow on hands and knees. Twenty or thirty feet later I came into a tiny compartment about four feet square. A round hole barely big enough to admit me led up from it. Marvelous daylight streamed into the compartment.

I had stumbled into Fawn and Blackie's den. Fawn went up and out the hole. I followed and stuck my head out and looked around. The bright light of day hurt my eyes and I was conscious as never before of the whiteness of the snow, the blue of the sky, the Christmas-card look of snow-laden trees and bushes.

Blackie and Fawn stood about thirty feet away looking at me.

It took but a minute to figure out the meaning of the branch tunnel. The prospector, looking for a vein of gold, had dug this tunnel. Not realizing how close he was to ground surface, he had broken through and then abandoned it. Fawn and Blackie had found the opening a ready-made den for their young. Here was our way out. Now to get Mike here.

Mike lay as I'd left him. I knelt beside him and told him what I'd found. "We can get out that way if you can walk or crawl, or maybe I can carry you."

"Help me up, I don't think the rock hurt my legs."

I managed to get him up. He groaned once and cried out with pain. He leaned against the side of the tunnel, sweat beading his face. I worked his parka on, then put on my own and slung the rifles over my shoulder by the straps. I carried the torch in my right hand and got my left arm around Mike's waist. Mike put a hand against the tunnel wall to steady himself. He turned his head and spit out a mouthful of blood. In the light of the torch it had a ruby shine.

"Whenever you're ready," I said. "Take your time."

"All — right. Let's — try."

Mike moved one foot forward, then the other. He put a lot of weight on me. My arm around him lifted and steadied him. Mike groaned and retched at each step. His weight came more heavily on me. We made about ten feet, then Mike leaned against the tunnel wall panting, his eyes shut, lips bloody from the internal bleeding. He shook his head and murmured, "No — use. Can't — make it. You go on. Get — out."

"We came in together," I said. "We leave together. We made ten feet. There's only about eighty more to the big rock. We've got all the time there is. We're going to make it."

In the torch light I saw the pain in his brown eyes, in the sagging lines of his face. He tried to smile but it was only a stretching of his broad lips. "You're a bullhead," he whispered. "Quite — a — tiger. Okay, when you're — ready."

It was agonizingly slow. We stopped many times but finally reached the big rock. Mike was about to collapse and I had to hold him against the rock. "From here," I said, "it's hands and knees. You think that might be easier than walking?"

"Could — be."

It was. I crawled along behind him holding the torch so he could see. Mike did much better crawling. We made the den area in a matter of minutes. Mike murmured, "Never — knew how — good daylight — looked."

Mike rested in the den while I crawled outside to look for Hank and Emmitt. The exit was on the opposite side of the hill from the cave entrance, so if they were watching for us we were safe. Then I saw Fawn and Blackie near the top of the hill. If Hank and Emmitt were about, the wolves would not be up there in plain sight. I was sure now that Hank and Emmitt felt they had us safely buried and had returned to their cabin.

I returned to Mike and with much pushing and pulling got him out of the den. Mike lay on the snow panting, "More'n — a mile — to th' cabin. Can't — make — it."

"You're going to make it," I insisted. "We got this far. You've got a date with a pilot this spring to fly us out, and you've got an appointment with my father, and don't forget that Hilltop restaurant up in the hills you always wanted to take your wife to. You're going to keep those dates if I've got to drag you. And that's a promise."

The brown eyes, dark with pain, looked at me. Again he tried to smile and again it didn't come off. "When — you're — ready — tiger."

I knew it was slow, tortuous, and agonizing for Mike. We made countless stops to rest, and, each time, Mike left mouthfuls of blood on the snow.

The wolves came down off the hill and fell in behind us. It was odd to see them there adjusting their pace to ours. Perhaps they were following us back to the cabin for their handout of moose meat. But I had the odd feeling they somehow knew there was something very wrong and were watching over us. They stopped and moved in unison with us. They stayed about the same distance behind. Mike said, "You — don't have — to look — for Hank and Emmitt. Watch — the wolves. They'll — let — you know."

I watched the wolves and their attention remained normal and on us.

It took several hours, but there was still plenty of daylight when we reached the cabin. I got Mike on his bunk, his parka off, and began to build a fire. "No fire," he mumbled, "they'll see smoke. Dead — giveaway."

"We've got to risk it," I said. "I need hot water to clean you up and warm up the cabin.

"Hunt dry wood. No — pitch — no — bark."

I found what I wanted, lit the fire and put a big pan of snow on the stove to melt. Then I went outside to check. There was very little smoke.

Fawn and Blackie sat on their tails and patiently waited to be fed. I went to the cache, cut two big chunks of meat, and took them to the usual spot. I squatted in the snow before the wolves holding the meat. Both cocked their heads and looked at me, sharp ears forward, yellow eyes studying me. Fawn ran out her pink tongue and gave me her grin.

Once again I had the odd feeling that somehow they knew all was not well. Maybe they sensed my worry. Mike was badly injured and I didn't know what to do. I lived for each minute. I was afraid to think even an hour ahead. I was terribly alone. I was frightened for Mike. I didn't know what to do. I needed help. I needed a friend, someone to talk to. The only friends I had in the world sat calmly in front of me. So I talked to them.

"I wish I could tell you how much I appreciate your being here today. You saved both our lives. Without you we'd have died back in that mine tunnel. You've earned this feed today more than I can ever tell. Without you I'd never have made it this far. You have taught me an awful lot. Blackie, you've been a gentleman, a very dignified gentleman. Fawn, you're one of the greatest ladies I've ever known. Here are your lunches. It's not much for such special friends. Enjoy it."

I tossed the meat in front of them and I squatted there in the snow and watched them trot away, heads high, tails waving. Then I went back to the cabin.

I found an old tomato can Mike could use to spit in. Blood kept coming, red and thick. There was a frightening amount.

Finally the snow melted and the water was hot. I bathed Mike's face, found a few scratches, but nothing serious. I washed his neck, then opened his shirt to look at his chest and stomach. Shock rolled through me and I knew how badly Mike was injured. His chest looked caved in, as if every rib were broken. The flesh was blue and ugly. I began gently to wash the dirt away but Mike stopped me. "Let — it go," he murmured. "It — hurts — too much. Won't do — any good."

"It'll help," I insisted. "You'll feel better and I'll be better able to help you."

Mike shook his head, "Face it — tiger — I know. This — one — you — can't win. I won't — keep — that appointment with — the bush — pilot — or your dad. Right here's — end of — the line." He was silent a moment as if gathering the strength to go on. Then he murmured, "Funny — always felt — I'd never — go back."

I swallowed a couple of times before the words would come. "You're going out with me. I'm not letting you off the hook. You hear?" But I felt there was little conviction in my voice.

Mike did manage a wan smile then. "Have it — your way — tiger."

"Would hot towels on your stomach and chest ease the pain?" I asked.

"Might."

I wrung out a towel and draped it carefully across his chest and stomach.

"Feels good," he said. "I'll rest some."

I stood looking down at that long, tough body, broken now. I remembered the day Mike had found me, the long miles the big man had brought me to his cabin. I thought of the miles he'd traveled during a cold Alaskan night to get me when I ran away to join Hank and Emmitt. Mike had saved my life then, too. I thought of the fight in their cabin the day Fawn was shot. As a team we'd given them both a first class beating. Mike looked almost delicate now. I wouldn't have believed such a thing could happen to Mike Donovan. He always seemed too indestructible. Now pain lines etched his rugged cheeks. His skin had a bloodless, pasty look. The sweat of great pain beaded his forehead. I wiped it away. He didn't open his eyes. Standing there watching him, an all-consuming rage boiled up in me.

Then and there I came to a decision. It was not a sudden decision. I realized it had been forming, growing ever since the cave-in. But only these last minutes had it hardened into a irreversible fact. I made it with my mind clear, cold, and deliberately calculating.

Mike had once said that up here, on the rim of the world, you dropped back in time a hundred years. All things became elemental, eating, starving, living, dying. Men made their own laws and lived by them. Just today he had jokingly called me "tiger." All right, I'd be one. Like that greatest of all predators who waits patiently beside a game trail for the victim to appear, I, too, would wait.

As soon as I had Mike resting comfortably I was going to pay Hank and Emmitt a visit. I'd not go rushing in as Mike had that time. I'd wait outside, behind the very tree from which I'd watched them load the furs in the chopper. This time when they stepped outside the door there'd be no hesitation. I'd kill them both.

- 14 -

I continued to put hot packs on Mike's chest and stomach and they seemed to help. As soon as he quieted down I'd leave for Hank and Emmitt's.

The time finally came. I stood beside the bunk and studied Mike carefully. He seemed to be sleeping. His breathing was shallow but even. I filled the stove with wood, closed the damper, took up the three-hundred and was ready to leave.

The moment I opened the door a shot smashed into the wood alongside my head. I slammed the door and drove the bolt home. My mind raced back to the day Ross and I arrived and the sound of shots striking the plane. I was sure it had been Hank.

From the bunk Mike's pain-wracked voice asked, "What happened?"

"Hank and Emmitt are here."

Mike motioned me closer, "Figures." His voice sounded a little stronger. There weren't the long pauses between each word. "They thought they had us safely — buried. They've come to ransack the cabin. Rifles here, gear, grub, stuff from the sled wreck, a few furs. Where are they?"

"I got one quick look as I slammed the door. They were walking up in plain sight. Hank let go with that quick shot, then they ducked into the brush."

Mike coughed and said, "Must have been a shock — learning we got out."

"What do we do now?"

Mike was quiet a moment. Then he murmured, "That's a real tough problem. Didn't figure on this." He was silent again, his breathing a rough sound in the cabin. "I — I'll think on it."

I sat on the bench beside his bunk and tried to think of something we could do. All I could think of was to stay as we were and I'd try to fight them as best I could. But they had a definite advantage. The second I opened the door they knew exactly where I was. They could be anywhere out there and they only had one place to watch — the door.

Mike lay utterly still staring at the ceiling. Once he turned his head and spit into the can, then resumed his staring. Finally he drew a slow, shallow breath and said, "If they knew I couldn't fight and was flat on my back — they'd take us in a hurry. Hank never overlooks — a bet. Got to make him think — I'm okay."

I looked at him lying there so crushed and still and asked quietly, "How do we do that, Mike?"

"Only one way. Help me sit up."

I got on the bunk behind him, placed my hands under his shoulders and gently pushed him upright. He emptied his mouth of blood and then sat bent over the side of the bunk. Finally, he muttered, "Button my shirt — so I look normal. And get me — a rifle."

"What're you thinking of? You can't go out there. You can't even walk."

"Not going out," he spoke slowly, as if fighting for breath between the words. "Gonna — fool 'em. Make 'em think we're both fine — are waiting for them. Help me — over in front of th' door. I'll use th' rifle — kind of a crutch. Help hold me up. Put th' butt — on th' floor and hang onto th' barrel. It's gotta look — normal. There much daylight left?"

"Quite a lot. It won't start getting dark for a couple of hours."

"Good." Again he just sat, head down, as if calling up the strength to speak. "Door faces th' light. Light'll shine into th' cabin — on me. Right?"

"That's right."

126

"Turn th' — lamp high. Get all th' light — we can. They've got to see me. They'll be about — a hundred yards off. No cover closer. Won't be able to see — what shape I'm in."

"What're you going to do?"

"Stand me in front of th' door — holding th' rifle. Open th' door — so they can see me. I'll look strong — healthy — ready to challenge them. I'm gonna yell insults — show them how ready we are. But be ready — to slam th' door. Won't be able to stand more'n a few seconds."

"How can you yell at them? You're practically whispering now. Your voice will give you away."

"Got a — better idea?"

"No."

"Then I'll try. Know those two. Nothing else we can do — will hold them off. If I put on a good act — might hold — 'em off for hours. They're not — anxious to tangle with us. We licked 'em once. Better shots than they are, too."

"If we hold them off for a little, what happens after that?"

"Maybe I'll think of somethin'. One thing — at a time. Now — get th' rifle — help me to th' door."

Mike leaned heavier on me than before, but I got him upright at the door. He stood, legs braced apart, holding the rifle by the barrel. His whole body was shaking. Sweat poured down his face. He spit blood onto the floor and said harshly, "Open th' door. Quick, open it."

I yanked the door wide and there he stood completely bathed in the last of day's light. He looked big, tough, indomitable. He looked like the man who'd beaten Hank senseless. Where he found the voice I'll never know, but suddenly it went booming out across the frozen tundra, full of power, confident, angry, taunting. "All right you two-bit bad men. What took you so long getting here? It's a good day to die, Hank. Come and get it."

He started to wobble. The rifle slipped from his hand. I slammed the door, shot the bolt and caught him as he started to fall. A pair of bullets tore into the door.

I half carried, half dragged him to the bunk and stretched him out again. His face was drained of color, his eyes black holes. His breathing was a tearing, ragged sound. He tried to smile and whispered thickly, "You — think this act rates an Oscar nomination?"

"If it doesn't, I'll complain to the board," I said.

"Do that," he whispered. "Maybe it'll hold 'em off for a while."

It held them off. I heard nothing and peeking through the window where I'd scratched the frost away and out a crack in the door, I saw nothing. But the cabin had only one window and there was no way to check the opposite and back walls. I was worrying about those walls when I heard the tiniest scratching across from the window. It sounded like a mouse. But we'd never had mice. Mike heard it, too. He lifted a hand and pointed. I tiptoed across the room, knelt and listened.

The gnawing seemed to come from about a foot off the floor at a chinked crack between two logs. Bits of moss and dried mud fell on the floor. Then the point of a knife blade came through. I tiptoed across the room and returned with the three-hundred. I showed it to Mike so he wouldn't be startled.

I knelt beside the working knife blade, silently eased back the bolt, pointed the muzzle straight through the crack and pulled the trigger. The explosion slammed against my eardrums. I jacked in another shell, moved the muzzle about a foot along the crack and fired again. There was a wild yell and the sound of running feet. I recognized Emmitt's voice.

Then all was quiet.

Night threw its cape over the white-encrusted tundra. A full moon climbed into the night sky. The stars came out. The snow became patterned with the ghostly shadows of trees and brush. The temperature began to drop and I felt it creeping into the cabin. I added wood to the stove and turned the lamp low. When I wasn't putting hot towels on Mike's chest and stomach, I watched the window. If Hank or Emmitt got one peak through the window and saw Mike, they'd know immediately the condition we were in.

I kept hoping for color to return to Mike's cheeks, his eyes to clear. It didn't happen.

I wondered if Hank and Emmitt had left or were still waiting. Then I wondered what they were waiting for. For us to run out of stove wood and the cold to drive us out in the hope they'd gone? For us to run out of food and have to visit the cache? But mostly, I was sure, for us to open the cabin door and expose ourselves.

Hank and Emmitt knew they had us trapped and it was just a waiting game. We'd eventually be forced to try something. We couldn't stay cooped up in the cabin more than a day or two. I wondered what was going to happen to Mike. All I could do was doctor him as we had Fawn, and his injuries were much worse.

I was standing near the window peering out at the northern night when Mike's pain-wracked voice said, "Joe."

I went to the bunk. Mike patted the side for me to sit down. His words were painfully measured. "Been thinkin'. We're — in — a mess. They got us stoppered even better — than in — th' mine. There's nothing we can do. They'll know soon — maybe by morning — something's wrong with me. Hank's smart. He'll figure it."

"Don't talk," I said. "Rest. We'll figure a way out."

Mike shook his head. "Not from this." He moved his big hands nervously. "I've thought — it through. Listen, don't argue. Not up to it."

"All right."

Mike rested. He seemed to be marshalling every ounce of strength he had left in that lean, once powerful body. When he finally spoke, his voice seemed stronger. The long hesitations between words and phrases were gone. "They can wait us out a day — a week. We've got to go through that door. All they have to do is be ready. Out the window's the only way."

"What about you?" I asked.

"I can't make the window. And if I did, I couldn't walk. And there's two hundred miles to go. I'm finished. If I was in a big hospital maybe they could do something. But I'm here. I know how bad I'm busted up."

"In a couple of days you'll feel better," I insisted. "We can hold them off that long."

For answer, Mike turned his head and spit into the can. It was pure blood. "Face it," he said. "The things you can change, you do. Those you can't, you accept. We save what we can. You're it. Even that's not sure."

I started to argue and Mike lifted a hand to stop me. "You're the one they're after. Not me. It's you they got to get — cause you can blow the whistle on them. I'd do it if I could get out, but I can't. Just listen to me. You're going to make that two-hundred mile hike out. You're going to do it alone. You can do it. You've got it in — here now." He tapped his chest. "I'll tell you what to do — to live. Listen good. Your life depends on it."

"All right." Mike was talking as if he knew he was going to die. I was almost crying.

"Go out th' window — tonight. The darkest part. Around two o'clock. Be sure you've got — your knife and matches. There's a roll of fishline on th' shelf. Take it. It can come in handy. You can make snares or fish. Don't shoot unless you have to. With luck you'll get a few hours head start. You've got to keep ahead. If they get ahead they can lay a trap for you. Remember — they're out to kill you. They don't dare let you get outside. You can inform on them. Keep ahead. Always keep ahead. Lose that lead and they'll trap you.

"Hank and Emmitt will know where you're heading. You can't shake them because there'll be your snow tracks to follow. Don't try to ambush them. There's two of them and Hank knows every trick."

Mike was silent a minute, then he continued. "It'll be two hundred miles. Hank won't try to catch you. He'll let you wear yourself out. You've got to be careful you don't. You can't take a day off to rest up. You've got to stay ahead, always ahead. You can win. You've got youth, heart, and you've got it up here." He tapped his head. "Use it. You've got to outthink Hank every day. Never mind Emmitt. He's nothing."

Mike rested again. "Take the three-hundred. It's light, powerful. It'll outshoot anything they've got. If they get too close, drive them back beyond range with it. Kill them if you have to, but only as a last resort. Killing any man is a terrible burden to carry.

"Head for the mountain range you can see from here. When you hit it, turn right. Keep the range on your left, it'll take you into civilization. Once you hit a town you're safe. They'll never follow you there." He gripped my arm with a strength that surprised me. His breath came short and hard. "Hunt up my wife when you get home. Tell her I'm sorry I doubted her — and that — I love her."

"I'll do everything you say but one," I said. "I'm not leaving you here alone. If — if it's like you say and you can't make it, I'm staying just as long — as long as you're here. That's final. I won't leave you alone, so don't ask me to."

Mike looked at me the longest time and finally he smiled. How he did it, I'll never know, but for one moment the pain seemed to be gone. It was the kind of smile I had seen the night we returned from beating Hank and Emmitt in their cabin and I had decided to stay. In spite of the pain and knowing what lay such a short time ahead, that smile was the most beautiful I have ever seen. It burned into my mind for all time. A smile I would cherish, that for the rest of my life I would measure other smiles and other people by.

Mike wanted me to begin getting ready immediately, but I just sat on the edge of the bunk and held his hand and Mike gripped mine as if he would never let go. Finally he asked, "Joe, you still here?"

"Of course." I squeezed his hand.

"It morning yet?"

"Not for hours. Do you want another hot pack?"

Mike shook his head. "Leave before morning. You've got to leave while it's still dark."

"I know. Rest."

A few minutes later Mike murmured urgently, "Lift my shoulders! Lift me up, Joe!"

I got on the bunk behind him, put my hands under his shoulders, lifted him, and held him against my chest. Blood

131

dripped from the corner of his mouth. Then he sighed softly and rolled his head against my chest.

I held him so for several minutes before I became aware of the utter silence. I put a finger under his chin and tipped his head up. In the dim lantern light I looked into the white face, the eyes, and I knew. "Mike," I said softly. "Mike, oh, Mike!"

Mike Donovan was dead.

I began to shake. I held him tight in my arms as I might have held a child, and a great loss went crying through me. I held Mike tighter and tighter as if I would never let him go. Finally the spasm passed. I tried not to think.

The fire burned out. The night's cold began to ooze through the walls. The coldness finally made me realize I had to leave while it was still dark.

I laid Mike down gently and covered him with a blanket. Then I just stood and looked at him. He seemed to be sleeping. My first thought was, he's free at last. Free of any feeling of guilt, free of this half-million square miles of prison he's been in for three years. I wanted to say something, but there was so much. So I just said, "Mike, you'll never know how much I'll miss you." Then I got my pack and sleeping bag and began packing the things he said I should take.

I had everything ready when I heard the sound. Mike had said it was getting late in the season for it. As always, it began as a whisper on the night, then swelled in volume to a clear, high call that flowed across the winter-locked tundra and filled every nook and cranny of the land. In it there was a note of sadness and longing and a kind of heartbreak I'd never heard in a wolf's voice before. It died away and for several minutes there was silence, as if the very night and every creature in the North waited.

There was no answer. The call was repeated again and again. Finally I put my head in my hands and began to cry. At long last the wolf lament ended and so did my tears. I was trying to figure some way to get the window out of its solid frame quietly when I smelled the smoke. I looked at the stove. It was all right. Then I saw the thin ribbon drifting up from the chinking between the logs where Emmitt had been working with the knife.

They had set fire to the logs from outside. I rushed over to try to smother the fire. Since it was outside, there was no way, and these bone-dry logs would make a roaring fire within minutes.

Behind me, the window glass shattered. A bottle of coal oil, the kind used for lamps, crashed to the floor and broke. Oil spewed across the floor. It had a lit wick that immediately ignited the spreading oil and half the cabin floor burst into flames.

I couldn't go out the door, they'd be waiting for me. I grabbed the three-hundred, pointed it out the window and sprayed the snow. If anyone was there, it would drive them away. I scooped up Mike's heavy rifle, jerked the door open and standing partially behind it, swept the surrounding snow. Then I caught up the pack, slammed it through the window and broke out the remaining glass.

The window was too high. I dragged the bench near, leaned the three-hundred against the wall, stepped on the bench and crawled head first through the opening.

Halfway through I reached back for the rifle. Something snagged the leather strap and held it fast. I yanked again and again. I tried to look inside, but the heat was too great. I thought of dropping back inside to unsnag it. But the moment I hit that flaming floor my clothes would be afire. I continued to yank, trying to break the strap. The glass-smooth barrel finally slipped through my mittened hand and it fell to the floor inside. Then I gave up.

I dropped into the snow, grabbed my pack, and darted into the surrounding brush. Behind me the night was torn apart as Hank and Emmitt sprayed the cabin with rifle fire.

They hadn't seen me climb out the window. That meant I'd get a head start for as long as it took the cabin to burn and for them to make sure I hadn't burned in it. I could have as much as a two or three hour head start.

I began to run. I tripped over limbs under the snow, over rocks and frozen mounds. I fell, rose, and ran again. I ran until my heart and aching lungs forced me to stop.

From the top of a low hill I looked back at the cabin several miles away. In the clear northern night the snow was tinted red by the flames. I could even make out Hank and Emmitt watching from several hundred feet away. Mike would be cremated by now. Then I thought of the wolves. They'd return for their moose meat feed tomorrow. But Hank and Emmitt would be on my trail by then. They'd be safe. I wondered how long they'd return to sit before the charred embers and wait. Not long, I hoped.

I began walking fast, heading straight for the great range that punched white and majestic into the night-blue bowl of the sky. I was finally embarked on the trip I'd wanted to make since the day Mike found me. But I was going alone, and without the rifle I so desperately needed. Hank and Emmitt would be coming fast, their incentive to catch me as great as mine was to escape. All I had for protection was the strength and speed of my legs, the bigness of my heart, and the sharpness of my mind. I wasn't sure it was enough. Mike had said with almost his last breath I would get through. I had to believe him.

It dawned on me suddenly that the direction I'd taken would pass within half a mile or so of Hank and Emmitt's cabin. The thought hit me so suddenly I stopped while it worked its way through my mind. Hank and Emmitt were waiting for our cabin to burn so they could check to see if I was in it. When I wasn't they'd hit the trail and be right after me. Following my tracks they'd arrive where I now stood — a half mile from their cabin. Naturally they'd stop long enough to stock up on food, sleeping bags, and whatever they needed for the trek to catch me. Into that thought I could almost hear Mike's voice, "Deny them everything you can. Make it as rough on them as possible. Burn them out, Joe. Do it now, immediately! You've got the time. Take it!"

It took maybe twenty minutes to reach their cabin. Their cabin was about the size of ours, only newer. The first thing I looked for was an extra rifle. There was none. Their oil lamp hung from the ceiling by a rope.

I stood on a bench and cut the lamp loose. Then I upended it, poured the coal oil across the floor, and lit it. I left the door open as I left, watching as flames leaped across the floor and up the walls.

- 15 -

It was several hours later when I stopped on a high rise of ground to catch my breath and rest. From here I watched the new day sweep down off the distant peaks and fan out across the tundra. Down there a moose lumbered into view and wandered about feeding on tender shoots. A fox darted through the low scrub chasing a snowshoe rabbit. It caught it, killed it, and made off with its prize.

My back trail was a plain thread in the snow. There were no following dark figures, but I knew there soon would be. I studied the distant mountain range that Mike said would take me into civilization. I guessed I'd traveled about eight miles. One hundred and ninety-two miles to go.

I started off again.

The sun was about halfway across the bowl of the sky when I made my first long stop. I was ravenously hungry. I sat on a rock, opened a can of beans, and ate. I ate handfuls of snow for water. I'd hold the snow in my mouth until it melted, then swallow. It was not as satisfying as a real drink, but it served.

I entered a large section of timber that took more than an hour to work my way through. I lost track of the mountain range and hoped I was traveling in the right direction. When I finally emerged and looked up, there it was, right where it should be.

It took the remainder of the daylight hours to reach the rolling foothills. Traveling became harder. I hiked uphill a lot and these hills were split by ravines and canyons. In some, snow had drifted six and eight feet deep. I had to hike above or below the ravines. That slowed me down.

The moon and stars came out. The night was almost as bright as day. I walked as long as my legs would carry me. Finally I found a spot where the butts of two trees had fallen close together and formed a protective hole between them. I swept the hole clear of snow with my hands, spread my sleeping bag, and crawled in.

I was bone-tired but sleep would not come. I listened to the soft whisper of the wind and thought of Mike and of Fawn and Blackie. The terrible sense of loss was almost more than I could bear.

Some small animal clawed at one of the downed trees and that sound telegraphed to me. An owl called eerily into the silence. A flying night bird trailed its voice across the tundra. I thought of the distance I'd traveled, the unknown miles yet to go. No wonder Mike had refused to take me across this land. I had eight cans of beans left, about three pounds of dried moose meat. And there was almost two hundred miles of back-breaking travel ahead. I had to ration myself sternly and be on the lookout for other food. Thinking of that I finally slept.

I was hiking again before dawn. I was hungry, but I held off eating as long as possible. Below, the frigid world lay still. Far as I could see nothing moved. The only sound was the soft swish of my feet through the foot-deep snow.

An hour later the night had spent itself. Morning light spread thinly across the folded hills, the valleys and draws, and across the great expanse of flat tundra. The sky became a cloudless, cobalt dome stretching from horizon to horizon. The stars faded. The cold, silent day was upon me.

From a high ridge I looked out across the ice-locked land searching for some small movement against the snow's whiteness. There was none. I was still well ahead of Hank and Emmitt. But out there, leading back were my tracks as far as I could see. If there was only some way to erase my tracks.

An hour later I was resting on a log when a dozen caribou rounded the brow of a hill and went charging away. A pair of wolves followed in their wake. They were all headed the direction I must go. I got into their tracks and followed. Looking back, mine were lost amongst theirs and it was much easier walking. I followed until they cut down onto the flats. A couple of miles further I came on moose tracks going my way. I followed them for some distance. It wouldn't fool Hank and Emmitt long, but it would delay them some hunting out my tracks from the animals'.

I spent the night in the lee of a rock. The one can of beans I allowed myself was little to travel on. I'd eaten a lot of snow to compensate for food. But it didn't help. I spent a miserable night with stomach cramps and visions of food — mountains of French fries and hamburgers.

Again I was up and hiking before daylight. The first thing, as always, I checked my back trail. Hank and Emmitt's whereabouts was beginning to worry me. Mike said they'd know where I was heading. Then maybe there was some shortcut they knew that would put them ahead where they could choose an ambush and lay for me.

From the edge of a grove of trees I studied the land I'd crossed. There, in the first of night's faint shadows I saw them no more than a mile away. I could even make out Hank in the lead.

I took off through the trees traveling my fastest. When I finally stopped to catch my breath, I thought of Hank and Emmitt. There was something different about them. Then I had it. They carried no packs. They had no regular sleeping bags. Of course, they had burned up when I torched their cabin. They were stripped down for the fastest kind of travel and I had stripped them down. With my pack and sleeping bag and the little food I had, I was carrying about twenty pounds more than they were.

I could not afford that handicap. My clothing was warm enough to sleep in. If they could do it, I could. I unslung the sleeping bag, packed the remaining cans of beans and moose meat in my pockets. I hid the sleeping bag behind some rocks, piled more rocks over it until it was hidden. I even took the shells for the three-hundred from my pockets and threw them away. I told myself it was easier traveling. It had to help some. Every ounce I could eliminate was bound to help.

I didn't see them the remainder of that day or the next. At night I tried to spot their campfire glow. But Hank was smart. If they had one, it was hidden behind a rock or in a grove of trees. I did hear them shoot again. The shot told me they were not as far behind as I'd have liked — and they were eating better.

So the days passed. I kept ahead, but I was getting steadily weaker. One can of beans and two pieces of dried moose meat were not enough. I tried to supplement this meagre fare with other food. I threw hundreds of rocks, and lost precious time, before I finally knocked over a rabbit. That night I had my first fire in days as I roasted the rabbit on sticks. The next day I got a ptarmigan with a long stick, literally knocking it out of the air. Again I had a small fire behind a big rock.

Then I went hungry two days. My aim on rabbits was bad and the ptarmigans were too far away. I stopped to rest more often. For the first time I saw the glow of Hank and Emmitt's night fire far below. They were gaining.

In another day or so they'd be in rifle range and this race would be over. That fire right out in the open told me Hank knew it. I'd gone about as far as I could. I was mildly surprised I could think about my own end so calmly. I guess it showed how close to exhaustion I was. I'd heard another shot that day. They were probably cooking another ptarmigan or rabbit. The thought made my mouth water, my stomach cramp.

I spent the night on the uphill side of a downed tree, but I did not sleep. I was hiking again early next morning. It was hard to get up, achingly hard to make my legs work. Sometime today, I told myself, but I wasn't going to stop and wait for it. They'd have to catch me.

I came into a game trail that was lightly packed and followed it. The trail skirted the side of a mountain and finally entered a large grove of trees. I was well into the trees when some sixth sense caused me to glance back. Hank was just coming into view. His head was down, intent on following my prints.

I began to run, stumbling blindly down the trail. I charged straight into a tangle of low-hanging limbs and brush. They whipped and snapped and scraped. Snow showered down. I knew Hank would hear and glanced back just as Hank looked up. He jerked up the rifle and fired. A sharp turn in the trail momentarily took me from sight. Hank was coming, long legs churning and shouting at the top of his lungs. "Emmitt, over here! Over here!"

The trail was crooked. The packed snow made for faster running. Where I got the speed I don't know, but I was keeping ahead of Hank. The trail took me around trees, rocks, mounds of earth and snow. Ahead of me some springy sort of tree was bent almost double over the trail, its limbs drooping almost to the snow. I dodged around it and raced on. I stumbled into a straight, open stretch of trail where I'd be visible to Hank and tried to increase my speed. It was no use. My tired legs were giving it all I had when there was a shout behind me. I glanced back, then came to a complete stop.

The limber tree had sprung almost straight and was shaking wildly. Hank was hanging from it upside down, head almost touching the snow, legs churning wildly. I could see some sort of wire or rope wrapped around his foot and ankle and he was yelling at the top of his lungs, "Emmitt! Emmitt! Get me down! Emmitt!"

Some trapper had set an animal snare in the trail. Hank had tried to duck under the tree and had stepped in the loop and sprung the trigger. The tree snapped erect and now Hank hung upside down yelling for help.

I thought of dashing back and getting Hank's rifle, but Emmitt came racing down the trail to Hank's rescue. I dashed on and disappeared around a bend. I heard Hank yelling for some distance.

I ran for several minutes, then slowed to a fast walk. It was going to take time to cut Hank down without some kind of wire nippers. I should be a couple of miles ahead by the time they were ready to take up the pursuit. I wondered how they had closed the gap on me without my knowing. Then I thought of my own physical condition. I had been ravenously hungry for hours. My legs felt ready to cave in. Therefore I was traveling much slower and hadn't been aware of it. If only I had the three-hundred, I could drive them back beyond the range of their smaller rifles. Even Hank's rifle, if I could have got it, would have given me something to fight with.

It was early afternoon when I finally came onto the cabin. It was a typical trapper's cabin, small, almost square, with a foot of snow on the roof. It sat almost hidden in a grove of trees.

I went down to it, lifted the latch, and went in. There was a dirt floor, a crude table with a bench, a small stove, a few pans on the wall, and a bunk in the corner. Shelves above the stove held a few boxes of dry food. Two pancakes lay in a tin plate on the shelf. A frying pan on the back of the stove held a slab of fried meat. In a corner leaned the greatest prize of all, a huge, gleaming powerful rifle. I lifted it and worked the bolt. It was loaded.

I fondled the rifle, stroking the gleaming stock, the slender barrel. I sighted through the long scope. I examined the inscription on the side. Dad had such a gun. Mike's big rifle was such a weapon. With this gun I could drive Hank and Emmitt far back out of range and keep them there.

With the rifle in one hand I made a sandwich of the meat and pancakes and began to eat. I had never tasted anything so good. I had just finished the sandwich when the door opened and a short, stocky man with a full beard came in.

He closed the door, leaned against it, and studied me. When he spoke his voice was heavy, neither friendly or unfriendly, and not very surprised.

"Well, I didn't expect company. You lost, boy?"

I shook my head. "I'm walking out."

"You mean to some town or somethin'? From here? You know how far it is?"

"Pretty far, I guess. I've been walking for days."

"Days? Where you from, boy? There's nobody but me in miles. How come you're here? And point that rifle someplace else. It's loaded."

I hadn't realized the rifle was pointed at his middle. Now the man's words gave me an idea. I kept the rifle aimed at his middle and made my voice determined, threatening. "Put your gun on the table and back away from it."

The trapper said, "If this's a joke...."

"No joke." The bolt made a dry click as I pulled it back.

The trapper carefully laid his rifle on the table, backed off a step, and partially raised his hands. "This is crazy. Just take it easy, sonny," he soothed. "I got no gold. I'm a trapper and this hasn't been a big year for fur. Anyway, you couldn't carry a lot of fur out to civilization. It's more'n a hundred miles."

"Not interested in gold or fur or in hurting you. I want to talk to you and I want to be sure you listen."

"Funny way to go about it."

"Just listen. You'll understand." I talked fast. I made it brief. Hank and Emmitt could be breaking down the door within the hour. I told the trapper how I came to be in the North, about Mike Donovan, Hank and Emmitt, the kind of men they were. How they'd killed at least one trapper for his fur and had probably been responsible for Ross dying and me being stranded. How they had trapped Mike and me in the mine tunnel. Why Hank and Emmitt were chasing me. "That's why I have to have this rifle," I finished. "They almost caught me this morning. Without the rifle, they're going to get me. With it, I can hold them off. You can see that."

"The thing I see," the trapper said, "is that you're sick."

"Sick!" I almost yelled.

"Cabin fever," the trapper said calmly. "I've seen it before. Just last year a trapper I know got the idea his friend was out to kill him. He snuck over, hid outside his cabin, and when he stepped outside he killed him. That's th' kinda sickness you got. Been alone too long you start imaginin' things."

"You're crazy," I almost yelled in frustration. "You're the one's been alone too long. And keep away from that rifle."

The trapper continued patiently, as if he hadn't heard, "Just think about it, boy. I never heard of no Mike Donovan. There's no place around here you could come from. No cabin, no nothin'. Never heard of no Hank or Emmitt, or killin' some trapper for his fur. Come off it, boy. I know cabin fever when I see it and you've got it bad. Put the rifle down. I'll take you to my main cabin. I've got short wave there. I'll call out a plane to take you to th' hospital."

"Can we leave now?"

"In th' mornin'. It's too late now."

"But Hank and Emmitt could come any minute."

"Boy," the trapper said patiently, "there's no Hank and Emmitt." He tapped his head. "It's all up here. B'lieve me."

There was no use talking further. I said, "I'm leaving and I'm taking the rifle with me. You got any more shells?"

"No."

"I think you have." I could see stubbornness in the trapper's chin, the tightening of his lips. I lifted the rifle purposefully and said quietly, "Don't make me do it."

The trapper shook his head, then reached behind a coffee can and tossed a box of shells on the table.

"You got a pencil or something to write with?"

"No."

"Then tear a piece out of that paper sack on the shelf and use one of the shells. The slug is lead and will do. Write your name, address, and what you want for the gun. I'll send you a check as soon as I get home."

The trapper wrote, handed me the paper and I stuffed it in my pocket along with the shells. I picked up his rifle and ejected the shells.

"What you gonna do with that gun?" he asked. "I need it."

"I know," I said, "but I can't take a chance of you using it on me." I thought a minute and said, "I'm going to toss it up on the roof of your cabin. You can get it, but it'll give me time to get away from here. I can't take a chance on you." I backed to the door. "This Hank and Emmitt will be following my tracks and may come here. Just remember, I've told you the truth, so be mighty careful around them. I'm going to try to lead them away from here. I'll do what I can."

I closed the door and tossed the rifle far up on the ridge of the cabin.

I followed my tracks back up to the point where I'd turned and gone to the trapper's cabin. I scuffed my feet through the

142

snow trying to obliterate my tracks down to the cabin. Back at my original starting point I turned sharp right, took up my original tracks again, and went on.

The pancakes and piece of meat had poured new strength into my tired body. I made good time through the short northern daylight hours. The heavy rifle did slow me a little, but the security and confidence it gave me was more than worth it.

I climbed away from the tundra. It was not quite dark when I came out on a rocky ledge that jutted from the side of the mountain. From the lip of the ledge it was a sheer drop of several hundred feet to the tundra below where the thread of my tracks disappeared into sparse timber. Here was a perfect place to watch for Hank and Emmitt. The sooner they knew I was armed the better. I sat in the snow at the edge of the lip, rifle cradled in my arms, and waited.

The day faded. Night spread its patterns of shadows over me and fled down the drop-off to the lower tundra. The air became colder. The stars emerged. Shadows made by the tree clusters dimpled the lower snow blanket.

How they got there without my seeing them I don't know, but suddenly in the thin screen of trees down there a campfire blossomed.

It was not big, but it would give them heat, and they could cook over it. They hadn't taken care to hide it. But then, why should they? They thought I was defenseless. They had almost caught me this morning. Tomorrow they surely would.

I moved along the ledge for a clearer view of the fire. Through the scope I made out two large blobs near the flames. They could be rocks or Hank and Emmitt hunched over the fire soaking up the warmth. If they were rocks, where were Hank and Emmitt? I moved the scope about but found nothing else near the fire. Those hunched-up looking blobs had to be Hank and Emmitt.

I could get one of them easily. Maybe both. I put the scope on the bigger blob. That would be Hank. He deserved to die, I told myself. He was responsible for Mike's death. They had killed others I knew. How many previous crimes they'd committed I

143

could only guess at. I pulled back the bolt and settled myself. This was an easy shot. It was then I remembered Mike's last advice. I could hear his voice as plain as if he stood beside me. "Kill them if you have to, but only as a last resort. Killing any man is a terrible burden to carry."

I listened and thought. This was not a last resort. The rifle changed that. What I really wanted was to get back to civilization, tell the authorities, and let them take Hank and Emmitt from there. Mike would agree this was the right decision. But I must startle them some dramatic way. They must realize I was not defenseless. That I could kill them and would.

I shifted the scope to the leaping flames. It was not even a difficult shot. I was shooting down so I wouldn't even have to allow much for the bullet dropping. For the maximum effect I had to hit that fire dead center. I drew a long breath and let it out. I drew another and held it. The rifle was rock solid in my hands. The leaping flames filled the scope. Slowly I pressed the trigger.

The explosion rocked the night and echoed against the towering mountains. Below, the fire suddenly shot outward in a dozen leaping tongues of flames. Startled yells drifted up. The two blobs became men scrambling wildly for cover. One portion of the fire still burned merrily. I ejected the spent shell and aimed at the remaining fire. With the shot, it scattered and died.

There was utter silence.

I searched for another target. I thought I saw a foot sticking out from behind a rock. I put a bullet within inches of the foot and it was jerked out of sight. Then I knocked a chip off the top of the rock. A stocking cap was lying in the snow. I put a bullet through it. I shouted down at them then, "The next time I'll put them dead center. You can count on it."

I moved back from the lip, made my way along the trail a hundred yards, then cut sharply right and began following the course of the mountain.

I hiked several hours, then burrowed into the snow at the foot of a tree and slept till dawn.

- 16 -

The rifle was the gift of life. With it, I drove Hank and Emmitt back well beyond the range of their lighter rifles. And it was also a source of food. I had twenty-five shells — five in the rifle and twenty in the box. Enough to see me into civilization and make sure I didn't starve.

I shot a big, fat ptarmigan the next day, taking its head off cleanly. I didn't mind that Hank and Emmitt heard me shoot. It was a constant reminder that I was armed now and was better with a rifle than they were. The next day I found a rabbit hanging dead and high from a sprung snare. I cut it down and took it with me.

I no longer hunted out the thickest timber or biggest rocks to keep away from Hank and Emmitt. Now I deliberately sought open stretches of tundra because they would have to cross them to keep track of me. With the rifle I tempted them to show themselves. In a sense I was now the hunter. They knew it, too, and tried to be cautious.

Twice I crossed open stretches, then lay in wait for them on the far side. Once I glimpsed them in the distance studying the open stretch and wondering if it was safe to try. I let them get halfway across where they stopped to rest. Emmitt was leaning against the side of a rock. I put a bullet within inches of his face, burning him with chunks of flying rock. The second time I cut a limb just inches above Hank's head. The limb fell, showering him with snow and making them duck behind trees.

One day I found a clear pool of water in a depression on top of a rock and drank my fill. It was the first good drink of water I'd had in days.

The pool, I suddenly realized, was the tip-off to approaching spring. Mike had said spring would come with express train speed. It did.

The air turned balmy, and even at night I was warm and comfortable. Snow melted off the ridges and hills and patches of yellow tundra appeared. The earth became soft. Melting snow water, unable to soak into the permafrost, seeped across the land and gathered in low spots forming lakes. The first ducks arrived while there was still ice on many of the ponds. Great V's of geese went over, their happy gabbling filtering down as they headed further north. I still ate well, though not as much as I'd have liked because I was trying to conserve my ammunition. A ptarmigan or rabbit lasted me two days.

I never lost track of Hank and Emmitt, though now I got only a few distant glimpses of them. They were like bulldogs, hanging on, waiting for some kind of break. They got it a couple of days later.

I skirted the base of a hill and started across a stretch of rolling, soggy tundra dotted with potholes and low draws where run-off water from the higher hills had settled. I detoured around them until I came to a particularly large one that wandered between two hills for three or four hundred yards. It was only about forty or fifty feet across, and tapping it with the rifle butt, seemed solid. There was no use walking around this soggy mire.

I stepped out on the ice and started across. I reached about halfway when something caused my feet to fly from under me and I went down flat on my back. My full weight suddenly hitting the ice broke it. I crashed through into a black, ice-cold world. I fought frantically to the surface and caught the edge of the ice. It broke. I tried again and again and it continually broke. Finally it held and I inched myself on top and crawled to shore.

I got to my hands and knees and began searching frantically. The rifle was gone. Then I remembered. As I hit the ice it was jolted from my hands. It was lost somewhere on the bottom of that mucky, black world. It was beyond finding some eight or ten feet down.

I was suddenly back where I'd started, a man without a gun. A tiger with his teeth and claws pulled. Once again I'd have to depend on my legs from here on. I took the remaining shells from my pocket and looked at them. You might as well join the rifle, I thought, and tossed them into the water. I brought out the bottle of matches. They seemed all right. I looked at the black water hole. There was nothing to hang around here for. I turned and walked away.

Luckily I'd eaten well while I had the rifle and my strength was up to normal.

I had to get my clothes dry while the daylight hours were still warm. I hunted up a section of thick brush, built a fire and stripped off my clothes. I hung them over the fire on sticks, then watched them like a hawk until they were dry. By that time it was dark and I stayed there the rest of the night.

For two days I kept ahead of Hank and Emmitt. But all I had to eat was the last half of a rabbit I'd shot. Then I went hungry. I finally got another ptarmigan with a rock and I found some high bush frozen berries that looked and tasted like cranberries. This carried me over another day.

That night I found a cave on the slope of a snow-bare shale rock hill. If I hadn't been looking directly at it in the early dusk I'd never have seen the small opening. It was overlaid by a huge slab of rock and the hole beneath was just large enough to crawl into. It might once have been a wolf den.

Inside I could almost stretch full length. I piled smaller rocks across the opening practically closing it. I felt so secure I was sure Hank and Emmitt could stand on the slab and never guess I was less than a foot beneath them.

It almost happened.

Voices woke me. I peeked between the rocks and Hank and Emmitt were less than thirty feet away looking out over the tundra, talking.

Hank was saying, "I'm bettin' he's around here, close. He can't travel no faster'n we can. The last couple days we been really steppin' it off. Really steppin' it off. He was gettin' mighty tired days ago when he ditched th' sleepin' bag. He'd never done that if he wasn't about played out."

"He got a rifle someplace," Emmitt said. "He's had things his own way since. Where'd he get it?"

"That trapper of course," Hank said. "There's somethin' mighty funny about that."

"Whatcha mean, funny?"

"Stop an' think, Emmitt. For days he's held us off, way outa range by shootin' our fire, shootin' close. We've had to stay way back. We ain't heard a shot from him now in almost a week. Not to get game, not to keep us back."

"Maybe he's runnin' low on shells."

Hank shook his head, "I don't think so. He's a smart kid. He figured how many he could use, and for what, and he was usin' 'em. Then, suddenly, he quit."

"Maybe he lost th' gun, or somethin'," Emmitt suggested.

"That's what I'm thinkin'. That place where he tried to cross th' ice, remember? We followed his tracks in th' mud right up to th' ice, then we seen his tracks on th' other side of th' water. And we could see where that ice had been broke through. I'm bettin' he went out on that ice, broke through an' when he did, he lost th' rifle. I'll bet that's what happened. It wasn't no animal fell through like we first thought. Since then he's had a couple of perfect places to wait an' take us and he ain't done it. I've got a feelin' he ain't got that rifle anymore."

"How we gonna prove that?"

"Don't have to. Th' fact he ain't shot at us is proof."

"But s'pose we don't come up with him, Hank? I'm gettin' kinda tired. Ain't you?"

"Sure, but we got to get him. You know that. I've got it all planned, Emmitt. How many times I told you you've got to look ahead? You gotta know th' fellow you're after."

"What do we know we didn't before?" Emmitt asked.

"He's a mighty tough kid," Hank answered. "But toughness will carry you just so far in this country. From now on he goes hungry most of th' time.

"Luck'll take you just so far. Not two hundred miles. He was lucky when he got that rifle. But that luck won't hold if he's lost it. I'm bettin' he has. He's gonna get weak, Emmitt. We can start closin' up on him now. Pretty soon we'll catch up with 'im.

When he's played out. Quit worryin'. Have patience. I told you we'd get Donovan, and we did. We'll get th' kid, too."

"Okay, if you say so," Emmitt said.

They went down the hill and disappeared into the trees. I waited some time and then crawled out. They had gone the direction I must take. Now I was behind. I didn't like that. They'd been closing on me the past couple of days and I wasn't aware of it. Luckily the snow was melting fast and had left great bare patches which I'd been following. Somehow Hank and Emmitt had lost my tracks. They could not know exactly where I was or they'd have had me just now. But what had worked for me was now working for Hank and Emmitt. I was behind and I could not pinpoint their location by their tracks, which had already disappeared in the spongy ground.

I sat on a rock, thought of Hank's assessment of me, and concluded he was right. As Mike had said, Hank was sharp. I hadn't realized the almost perpetual hunger I'd known since losing the rifle had slowed me down to the point they'd passed me while I overslept. Even after a night's sleep I was still tired. Hunger could be my undoing.

I went on, following the general direction Hank and Emmitt were taking. Now I had to search out ahead for fear of running into them. Fortunately, they were not yet aware they were in the lead. But Hank would soon figure that out. I had to regain the lead, but I wasn't up to traveling fast enough for a full day to do that.

I had nothing to eat that day and spent the night on the barren slope of a hill. A mile or so ahead I saw the star-shine glow of their camp fire.

Early the following morning I rounded the brow of a hill and saw two wolves feeding on the fresh-killed carcass of a large caribou. I found a club and with this I boldly walked toward them. Luckily, my association with Fawn and Blackie had erased much of my fear of wolves.

They stopped eating and studied me. They bared their teeth and began to growl.

I continued to advance, holding the club ready. I walked neither fast nor slow, but steadily. When I spoke I made my voice commanding, positive. "You've got more here than you can eat," I said. "I need some of it. One chunk, that's all. You can have the rest. But I'm going to have that piece. Now beat it. Go on, get out of here!"

For a moment I thought they might challenge me, but I kept advancing, brandishing the club. Their growls were harsh, rasping. One of them began clicking his teeth angrily. Suddenly the other began backing away a slow step at a time. After it had gone about ten feet the other followed. They both kept growling. I swung the club and yelled, "Go on! Beat it! Get out! Get!"

They trotted away, stopped after a couple of hundred feet and stood watching. I leaned the club against the carcass and got out my knife. It took but a couple of minutes to hack out a large chunk of choice meat. I looked at them, said, "Thanks," and walked off. The last I saw they were returning.

That night I hiked up the mountain slope almost a mile hunting a protected spot where I could build a fire that would not be seen. I found it at the bottom of a rocky cave, a cutbank. I gathered dry sticks that would not smoke, got a fire going, cut the meat into strips, and hung them over the flames to cook and dry. It took all evening and during the process I gorged myself. When I finished I cut a square of lining out of my parka, wrapped the meat in it, tied the ends and put it in my parka pocket.

I slept the remainder of the night and was hiking again before dawn. With a full stomach I felt stronger. I passed through a stand of scrub timber and was faced with a couple of miles of open, spongy tundra, then more forest. I studied this open, low land carefully. There was no way around. I'd be in plain sight. If they caught me in this open, I'd be dead. But I had no choice.

I stepped into cold, dirty water that oozed up around my ankles. Progress was slow. I kept my eyes on the wall of trees ahead, searching for any sign of movement. A moose came down to the water, drank, and wandered back into the trees. There was nothing else.

Finally I entered the trees and their cool protection. I'd been stung a few times by early mosquitoes. In another week or so this crossing would be murderous.

The ground here was solid, the hiking good. It was a big patch of woods and for more than an hour I made good time. Finally I came to a deep ravine and began following its edge looking for an easy way across. I was so absorbed in my search I wasn't aware of Emmitt until I almost bumped into him. Emmitt stood in front of me holding his rifle pointed at my middle and giving me that foolish grin. His colorless eyes showed no expression.

"You goin' anyplace special?" he asked in that whiny voice. Shock after shock rolled through me. My mouth was dry. My heart tried to jump out of my chest. My mind was filled with but one thought. The thing I feared most had come to pass.

Emmitt was enjoying himself. He still wore that stupid smile when he said, "We figured you'd be ten, fifteen miles ahead of us. Hank was right. You do look kind of starved down. And I see you lost your gun."

Then I began to think. My mind raced, looking for something, anything to trap Emmitt's attention. My hand touched the pocket where I carried the caribou meat tied in the piece of cloth. Looking into Emmitt's expressionless eyes and that silly grin gave me an idea. It was wild, illogical, but with Emmitt it might work. Hank wasn't here to take over the thinking. Emmitt was on his own. I wondered, briefly, where Hank was. They'd probably separated to search the ravine faster. I said, "You're pretty sharp, Emmitt. You figured out how to catch me."

"Sure," Emmitt smiled.

"Why do you kill people?" I was trying to lead Emmitt's thinking carefully, trying to hold his interest.

"Money in it. Good money."

"You like money?"

"Who don't? How come all this talkin'?"

"You and Hank had a chance to make a lot of money back at the mine when you caved in that entrance and trapped us."

"You got money?"

151

"Not me. But there was gold there. Lots of gold."

"You're crazy. That old man worked there for years. He never took out a dime."

"No, but he knew the gold was there someplace. Don't forget that's a gold mine, Emmitt. When you and Hank loosed that avalanche that blocked the opening, you exposed a big gold vein. Didn't you know that?"

"You're lyin'."

"I could be, but I don't have to. Here it is. I was taking it out with me." I carefully took the dried caribou package from my pocket. I stood tossing it gently in my hand. "All we had to do was gather it up before we left the mine." I held it up. "We weighed it back at the cabin. There's over three thousand dollars worth here. Pure gold, Emmitt. And you walked away and left it. You left it, Emmitt. There's lots more where this came from. Lot's more."

For the first time those pale eyes lit up. Greed was a naked shine.

"You can have this all for yourself, Emmitt. You don't have to split with Hank or anybody. Three thousand dollars in pure gold, Emmitt. But you have to let me go first. How about it?"

"Me and Hank always split. I wouldn't hold out on him." He held out his hand. "Toss it over."

"You let me go."

"If Hank says so." Then he shouted suddenly at the top of his lungs, "Hank, over here. I got him! I got him!"

I heard Hank's answer from a couple of hundred yards away. "Hold 'im. I'm comin'!"

I knew I'd gone as far as I could with Emmitt. "All right," I said. "You win. I should have known I couldn't beat you." I held out the sack and edged a step closer. Then another. And another.

Emmitt brought up the rifle muzzle. It centered on my chest. "That's close enough. Toss it over."

"Sure." I was within six feet of Emmitt. As close as I was going to get. I could hear Hank crashing through the brush. "All right. You win." Suddenly I tossed the sack straight at Emmitt's face. "Catch!" I said sharply.

Emmitt's free hand shot up automatically to catch it. The rifle muzzle wobbled. His greedy eyes were riveted to the sack. I launched myself feet first straight at his face. Emmitt tried to dodge. My driving feet slammed into his chest. Emmitt let out a startled yell. The rifle exploded. The bullet plowed into the ground. Emmitt went over backward and slid down the steep bank into the canyon. The rifle clattered down the slope after him.

I grabbed up the caribou sack and streaked through the trees. A bullet clipped a limb a foot or so from my head, then I was out of sight.

Both men were at least thirty years older than I and no match for me as a sprinter. I outdistanced them easily. I was ahead again.

I traveled fast the rest of the day and kept eating caribou meat. I needed the added strength. What I'd do tomorrow for food I didn't know.

Late in the day I crossed another open section of tundra. I looked back but saw no sign of Hank and Emmitt. Several miles further I came suddenly onto an old cabin in a grove of trees. I went in, found the usual table, bench, and bunk. Wood was laid in the stove. This would be a trapper's line cabin. Some trap lines were fifty miles long, so cabins were stationed along the way.

A shelf above the stove held two cans of food. One was tomato juice, the other vegetables. I punched a hole in the tomato can and tasted it. It was good. I drank it. The second can was carrots and peas. I ate that, too.

I buried the cans a mile or so away so Hank and Emmitt wouldn't get the direct line of my travel.

I spent the night under the edge of a log.

Next day I crossed a wide, swampy area where I sank almost to my knees. It was very slow going and this time the mosquitoes boiled up in clouds. I broke off a couple of budding branches and swirled them around my head but it didn't help much. I pulled the parka hood over my head and held it tight around my face, but they still got through.

Hunger was a devouring ache. I tripped over unseen roots and fell many times. Halfway across I was soaked from head to foot. It was a long two hours of hard, cold slogging before I finally emerged on the mountain slope where I could sit down and rest. I was so tired my legs wanted to cave. In spite of all the water I'd crossed, none of it was fit to drink.

I removed the parka, shook the water from it and put it on again. Then I just sat there, head down, too tired to move. I was so steeped in aches and pains I didn't hear the sudden rush of sound. I only became aware of the plane when its noise burst over me in a wave.

Here it came, shooting over the marsh, red, shining in the clear northern sunlight. Beautiful! It streaked over me. I watched, stupefied. It made a wide swing out over the land and water I'd just crossed and came shooting back.

Suddenly I snapped out of my trance. I leaped to my feet and raced to get into the clear — out from under the trees into the open. It was traveling very fast. I'd never make it. I stumbled and fell, jumped up, and plunged forward again. But I knew, that to the pilot looking down, the screen of limbs still hid me. I even glimpsed the man's face. Then the plane was gone.

I just stood there, sick, numb, discouraged, and listened to the sound fade away. Then the Arctic silence closed around me again as deep as unborn time.

- 17 -

I looked the direction the plane had disappeared and kept telling myself, "It'll come back. It's got to come back! In a minute it'll come roaring back over this muskeg and the pilot will see me!"

I stood out in the open, waiting. I didn't care if Hank and Emmitt did see me. Minutes passed, I don't know how many. The plane did not return. The sky was empty. The world was utterly empty. It had been a search plane, I was sure. They had covered this area and found nothing. They'd look somewhere else. No other plane would come. My one chance of being rescued was gone.

I sat down, completely discouraged. I'd come as far as my strength would carry me. I'd endured all the running, the cold, deep snow, freezing water, and mosquitoes I could stand. I was hungry, weak. My legs wanted to fold. At a guess I'd come a little more than a hundred miles. I was only about halfway — only halfway! Considering the shape I was in now, what chance did I have to finish this trek? Maybe I was lost anyway. I'd seen nothing to indicate there might be a town a hundred miles ahead. Maybe I'd got turned around somehow and was traveling the wrong direction, following the wrong mountain range. Stranger things had happened in the North. Mike was right. Two hundred miles was mighty long over country like this. I was so discouraged and beat I wanted to cry, but too many things had happened to me these past months. I was too big, too old, yes, and too seasoned by the country and the people I'd met to afford the luxury of tears. So I sat and wallowed in misery.

Why I should eventually think of it I don't know. But I could sense Mike's presence, hear his voice, and feel the power of his brown eyes as he'd looked into mine as he lay dying. "You're going to make that two-hundred mile hike out." He tapped his chest, "You've got it in here now." Then he touched his head, "And you've got it here. Use it."

Mike had never been wrong. Suddenly I could feel it rising in me like a flood, stubbornness, hope, an iron determination. It drove out despair, hopelessness, discouragement. It washed away doubt, fear, misery, and self-pity. Somewhere, somehow I'd find food. I'd done it before. I'd do it again. I'd keep putting one foot ahead of the other, and I'd travel those long, hard miles however many there were. I'd keep ahead of Hank and Emmitt.

I was going the right direction. I'd kept the line of mountains on my left. Dad had planes out, I was sure. If one found me, fine. If not, I'd still get there. But first things first. I needed food.

I found it the next two hours. I had passed through the trees and was crossing a barren stretch of tundra when a ptarmigan exploded out of the grass at my feet. I looked down and there, almost under my feet, was a nest with half a dozen eggs.

I knelt and felt them. They were warm. Ptarmigan eggs should be as good as chicken eggs. I cracked one. It looked good. It smelled good. I gulped it down. I ate all the eggs while the mother complained from a distance. Those half dozen eggs set me up again. I found nothing more that day and went to bed hungry at the base of a tree.

First thing in the morning I checked my back trail. There was no sign of Hank and Emmitt. But I knew that after my experience with Emmitt, they'd be more determined than ever.

I looked hungrily at big, fat geese. One of those would last days. But the geese were shy and stayed far out in the open water. While resting near a stream that formed a small lake I watched a fox entice a goose close to shore. The fox jumped about, went through all sorts of antics out in the open near the water. The goose, fascinated, came closer. The fox continued his odd capers.

156

The goose finally climbed out on the bank. That moment the fox dashed forward, caught the goose by the neck, and killed it with a couple of bites.

It started to drag the goose away. I was about to rush out and challenge the fox when two grizzly cubs galloped out of the trees and made for the fox. The cubs seemed to want to play. The fox was no match for them. They worried the fox until he finally left the goose and disappeared.

The cubs pawed and smelled the goose. I picked up a stick and ran to chase the cubs away. Here was good eating for a week. The cubs saw me coming and let out squalls of fright.

With a coughing roar a big mother grizzly burst from the brush and charged at me like an advancing tank. I sprinted for the nearest tree, scrambled into the branches, and climbed about twenty feet before I stopped. She reared against the trunk, jaws spread wide, growling and glaring up at me.

Finally she returned to the goose and I sat there for an hour while she ripped off the feathers and devoured it. Finally all three wandered away. I came down and hurried off.

Ducks were nesting on every water hole on the tundra. I searched for their eggs. I found plenty. Duck eggs are large and three was all I could eat at one time.

I was careful to keep a wary eye out for grizzlies and mother moose who were fiercely protective of their young. With the ptarmigan and duck eggs and an occasional fish I caught with the line, I made out fine.

The days grew warmer. The snow was almost gone. Small rivers and creeks were free of ice.

Each night I tried to estimate the miles I'd come, but it was impossible with the many detours I made. My guess was at least another forty or fifty miles yet to go.

Each morning I searched my back trail for Emmitt and Hank. I never saw them. At times I heard shots so I knew about where they were. It was too close for comfort. The fact Hank didn't seem to care I knew where they were worried me. It showed how confident they were. Did Hank know something? I wracked my brain trying to make sense of it but got nowhere. I had to keep my wits about me, my strength up, travel as fast as possible to stay ahead — and never panic.

The sixth day after the bear-goose incident, I was passing through a grove of trees when I heard a sound strange to this silent world. It was a little like thunder. It swelled in volume. Finally, as I advanced, I distinguished individual sounds. Sounds like falling or rushing water. Sometimes there were sharp reports, like rifle shots. Another, louder, sharper sound like falling or shattering glass.

When I emerged from the trees, there before me was the biggest river I had seen in the North. The spectacle facing me was heart stopping. I had heard and read about this phenomenon and now I was hearing, seeing it. The spring breakup of a big northern river.

The river was choked from bank to bank with moving, grinding, smashing cakes of thick ice. Some were as large as thirty or forty feet square and several feet thick. I watched, fascinated, as huge chunks reared suddenly into the air, forced upward by some underwater pressure, then toppled over on other floating pieces and shattered with thunderous reports. This and the grinding, smashing bumping of thousands of huge cakes made an awesome sound like I imagined cannonading in a war must be.

The mountain range I was following crossed the river and continued on. Somehow I had to cross this river.

Up ahead the river boiled out of a narrow gorge that sliced through the mountains. Maybe somewhere up there I'd find an ice jam or a series of rocks I could cross on.

It took more than an hour to hike into the narrow part of the gorge. Here, trapped between steep granite walls, the thunder of smashing, grinding ice was frighteningly loud. The maelstrom of white water was a boiling, churning, heaving millrace as far as I could see. I studied it for some minutes and then thought of Hank and Emmitt. Was this the reason Hank hadn't worried about catching up with me sooner? Did he know about this river and figured it would be in breakup and they'd have me trapped here on the river bank? I doubted it. But if it was, I had to give Hank more credit for being clever.

158

They didn't have me yet. Somewhere, somehow, I'd find a crossing. I returned downriver to where it widened out and the current slowed. I stood looking at the slow-moving ice and wondered how long it would take for the river to clear. A couple of days? A week?

Hank and Emmitt could pop out of the trees any time. Then it would be all over for me. The miles I'd traveled, all I'd been through, would be for nothing. This close! Thirty miles, maybe, to a town and safety. And yet so far! On the other side of this river that I could see across I'd be as good as home.

I hiked a mile or so downriver looking for anything that might help. I found nothing but a grizzly and her cub wandering along the bank scrounging for dead fish. There was no use going farther. As far as I could see the winding course of the river was the same.

I had to find a place to hide from Hank and Emmitt to wait for the ice to pass. Wherever I hid it had to be within sight of the mountain range I was following.

I was thinking about that when Hank and Emmitt stepped out of the trees a couple of hundred yards away and stood looking at the river.

I dove into the only cover close by — a tiny clump of bushes no more than two feet high. The only reason they didn't see me was because the wonder of the breakup held their attention.

After several minutes Hank began making motions as he talked to Emmitt. Watching, I understood what he was saying. They'd split up. One would go upriver, the other down. Hank knew I had to be here somewhere close. It was odd, the three of us trapped here together by the river. Hank knew that all they had to do was search carefully and they'd eventually flush me out.

Hank walked off upriver. Emmitt started toward me.

I waited as long as I dared, so Hank would get out of rifle range. Then I jumped up and began to run. I dodged among the huge rocks lining the river bank, giving Emmitt no clear shot. Emmitt fired once, the bullet chipping a rock several feet away. Then above the sounds of the river I heard Emmitt yelling, "Hank, over here! He's over here! Hank! Hank!"

I ducked around a couple more rocks and almost ran down the grizzly cub digging along the river bank. I'd forgotten about the bears. The cub let out a squall of surprise and fright.

There was a coughing roar up on the tundra and here came the mother in an all-out charge.

I whipped around another rock and Emmitt, coming after me full tilt, ran straight into the old bear's weak-eyed view. She took him.

I stopped behind the rock to look. Emmitt tried to stop and bring up his rifle. He slipped and almost fell. He got the gun up for one frantic shot. Then the grizzly was upon him.

She reared to hind legs and hit him a smashing blow with her paw. Emmitt collapsed screaming. The rifle went flying.

I watched in horrified fascination. Her huge jaws clamped on the back of Emmitt's neck. She lifted, shook him like a rag doll, threw him, and was after him again. Emmitt kept screaming. She hit him, dragged him, shook him, and pounded him with her paws. Emmitt's screams grew weaker and finally ceased. Still she dragged and bit and pounded him.

Hank raced down the riverbank, skidded to a stop, and fired two fast shots. I couldn't tell if either hit the bear. But she left Emmitt and with her cub at her heels ran off across the tundra into the trees. Hank went to Emmitt, turned him over, and looked at him. Then he raised his head and saw me. He jumped up and came after me, jacking a shell into the chamber as he ran.

I had a good start and my dodging among the big shore rocks gave him no good target. But I knew I'd run out of boulders in the next couple of hundred yards. Then it would be pebbly beach and I'd be a clear target.

I almost fell over a chunk of limb about four inches in diameter and four feet long. I snatched it up and ran on. What I'd do with it against a rifle I didn't know. But it was a weapon of sorts.

The last rocks were huge. Once I'd passed through them I'd be in plain sight. I ducked among them. At the last big one I whirled and crouched behind it. The river lapped at its base and several big chunks of ice were wedged there.

Hank charged through the rocks intent only on catching me. As he rounded the last one, I stepped out and swung the club at his head with all my strength.

Hank saw the club coming and threw up his arm with the rifle to ward off the blow.

The club crashed down on the rifle and knocked it from his hands. The gun splashed into the river.

The blow broke the club and I was left with only a foot of it in my hands. I threw it at Hank and missed.

The next instant Hank whipped out a knife. He pressed a button and a wicked seven-inch blade shot out. The way he held it, low down, pointed at my middle, I guessed he was no stranger to the weapon.

I backed up against the river, my feet in the water. Hank was big, lean, and surprisingly quick. There was no way I could get around him and the knife. Those black, hating eyes drilled into me. Then he lunged. I leaped backward almost knee deep in the river, turned, and scrambled onto the huge ice floe wedged there.

Hank was right behind me. He came at me in a crouch, holding the knife out. Those black eyes were fixed on me with an intensity I'd never known. Hank meant to kill me, or force me to jump into the river where I was sure to be crushed.

I backed to the lip of the floe and stopped. The roar of grinding, falling ice filled the air.

Hank's thin lips formed the words, "Now! Now!" The flashing blade darted like a snake's tongue. Hank swept it from side to side in lightening swift passes aiming at my stomach. Then he lunged.

On the ice he partially slipped. The lunge became half a lunge, half a forward fall.

I dropped to hands and knees on the ice. Hank went completely over me and I grabbed for his knife hand with both of mine. Hank's momentum and weight were too much. He slid off the ice floe into the river. I went with him, clinging to the knife hand as the water closed over us.

The water was liquid ice and seemed to freeze my muscles. We went to the bottom where the current rolled us over and over struggling in each other's arms. Then we were fighting our way up and I was clinging to Hank's knife arm with both hands. The moment we broke the surface Hank threw his free arm over the ice block to hold him up. I got a good look into those black eyes and they were wide with fright. Suddenly I realized Hank couldn't swim.

He tried to jerk the knife hand from my grasp, but he wouldn't take the other off the ice to help.

I was a good swimmer and now I had the advantage. I clung to Hank's right hand with my left and smashed my right fist into his face again and again. Hank would not let go of the ice floe to fight back. He ducked his face away and took the punches. But my punches had little effect. I jerked up my knee into Hank's stomach with all my strength. Hank gasped with pain. I brought the knee up again and again. Suddenly Hank dropped the knife and it fell into the river. He ripped his arm free and heaved himself onto the ice.

I came up almost beside him.

On the ice, Hank's size and strength told. He hammered me with both fists. The fear was gone from his eyes now. Only hate and determination showed. His lips were drawn back over his big, clenched teeth, his shoulders hunched. He knocked me down a couple of times, but I managed to avoid his stomping feet and scrambled up.

I tried to fight, but on the slippery ice neither of us did much damage. My head was ringing from the punches and finally to avoid them I dove head first into Hank. Locked in each other's arms we went sliding across the ice and fell. The fall jarred us apart.

We got to our feet the same instant. Hank was about to lunge at me...and then it happened.

In front of us, in a clear spot of water, a huge cake of ice reared out of the depths. It soared up and up, a good twenty feet above us, bright shining like a great diamond with the sun striking its clear surface. Then slowly, with majestic deliberation, it began to fall. It were coming down on top of the cake of ice on which we stood. There was only one place for me to go — back into the river.

I went off head first in a steep dive. Hank was standing, mouth wide in terror, hands above his head as if he would ward off the thousands of pounds that were crashing down upon him. I heard him scream as I went under. It was a thin, wailing, lost voice. An odd sound, I thought fleetingly, for such a big, tough man.

I headed for the bottom to get all the water possible over me. I thought I felt the concussion as the block fell. I got my feet on bottom, sprang upward, and began stroking for the surface again.

I came up in a small, ice-clear pool. I immediately looked for Hank. He was gone. The two huge blocks of ice had shattered into hundreds of small chunks that drifted about. I swam to a large chunk and hauled myself on top. Already the hole was closing as huge chunks crowded in.

As the ice packed in I jumped from cake to cake and worked my way quickly ashore. I sat on a rock shivering violently and looked at the churning, grinding ice. Hank was somewhere down there at the bottom of the river. His body might never be found. Emmitt lay on the tundra several hundred yards away, mauled and dead.

So quickly it happened, so quickly it was over. Less than three minutes of gunfire, of grizzly mauling, of fighting on the ice and in the river, and it was finished. There were only the sounds of the jam breaking the northern silence as the ice worked its way toward some distant sea.

Now I could take my time, wait for the ice to go out, then cross the river and go home. The suspense, uncertainty, the gut-knotting fears of months were gone. I was free!

I stood up. I was soaked from head to foot, but so great had been the excitement of the past minutes it didn't bother me. I was pulling off my parka to wring out the water when I became aware of a different sound. A sound that was high, sharp, insistent. I looked up and here it came.

A plane! A yellow plane with floats. It was shooting down-river not a hundred feet above the ice. It would pass right over me. I dashed into the water and began waving my arms and screaming at the top of my lungs. "Here! Here! Look down here! Down here!"

The plane roared over so low I could see two men in it. One leaned out the window, pointed a camera down, and took pictures. Then the plane made a wide circle and came back. It slowed to almost stalling speed and the cameraman leaned out and pointed ahead.

I looked, and there, less than a quarter mile away, was a small lake of clear water where they could land. I headed for the lake on a dead run.

The men were waiting on the bank when I arrived. "You a search plane?" I asked breathlessly.

"No. We're photographing the breakup. Anything we can do for you?"

"I'm Joe Rogers," I said. "I've been missing for months. My father's had planes out looking for me. I was hiking out."

"Rogers," the pilot said. "Sure, I remember. You came north with Ross Edwards. You and Edwards disappeared — cracked up or something. Your dad had half the North alerted and hunting for you. He made you something of a famous character up here. How about that. Hop in, we'll have you in town in a few minutes."

Less than an hour later I had Dad on the phone. "Dad," I said. "This's Joe."

"Joe?" Dad's voice was doubtful. "Joe?" he repeated. Then "Joel! Oh, my God. Joel!" The words poured out. "Where are you? How are you? Are you all right? Are you sure you're all right? I'll be right up after you."

I interrupted the torrent of words. "Dad, Dad. Calm down. Just listen. Listen, Dad. I'm all right. I'm fine. A bush pilot is taking me to Anchorage. They've loaned me the fare. I'll be home in a few hours. Then I'll tell you all about it. I've got to go now. We're about ready to take off." Then I just stood there, held the phone, and listened to that two-hundred and twenty pound ex-All American fullback and big-time lawyer cry like a child.

In the big airport at home I felt out of place, out of time. In my mukluks and parka I drew some odd stares and smiles. I felt crowded and jostled by people as I looked about for Dad. Then I saw him barging through the crowed, pushing people aside.

He stood before me, big as ever, tough-looking, indomitable as always. But there was a difference, a gentleness, a softness in his smile, in his voice, his eyes. "Joel! Joel! I've missed you." He reached for me, then his hands fell to his sides. "You've grown up!" There was surprise, wonder in his voice and a moment of uncertainty. "You're not a boy. You're a man! A young man!"

"Where I was," I said, "you grew up in a hurry or died."

"...I didn't realize what I was doing to you," he rushed on. "I've wished a thousand times I could tell you. I've so much to make up for...."

"There's nothing to make up for," I said. "Nothing to be sorry for. I had to grow up some. We go on from here."

Then I was almost crushed in Dad's big arms and he said in an emotion-choked voice, "Welcome home, son! Welcome home!"

Epilogue

Dad dropped the Joel and "Little" Joel and never used them again. Suddenly our relationship was the kind I had always wanted, the kind Dad and Rocky enjoyed.

Rocky was not home. He'd taken a job in the woods to toughen up for college football. I tried to find Mike's widow, but she had sold the company and moved away.

Dad and his partners had another pilot. Dad talked to me about flying North. He wanted to see the country, the very spot where I had lived. I wanted to go back. On a map I'd found the mountain range I'd followed. The very river where Hank and I had fought.

We could land on the creek bed half a mile from the cabin site. I wondered if Fawn and Blackie would be there, if they'd remember me. They'd have pups this summer. I'd take ten pounds of meat along just in case.

I wanted to stand by the ashes of the cabin, see it again in my mind's eye...and remember. Remember feeding the wolves, playing with Fawn. Remember the wolves bringing the frigid night alive with song. The lone wolf's mating call. The good talks Mike and I had. The wind whistling at the cabin's corners. The utter silence. Most of all I wanted to remember Mike's smile the night I decided to stay and fight beside him. His words, "You're quite a man. Yes, sir, quite a man!" That I wanted to remember most of all.

About the Author

Walt Morey packed enough real adventures into his life to be the subject of exciting reading himself. He worked as a boxer, construction worker, mill worker, shipbuilder, theater manager, and deep-sea diver. But it is as a superb adventure writer that young readers have come know him the world over. His love of nature and the wild runs like a great river through Walt's stories. The lives of his characters are woven into rich webs of outdoor suspense and excitement.

It's fortuitous that Walt came to write at all. Functionally illiterate until he was thirteen, he suddenly fell in love with books. Soon after, he discovered a desire to write. He practiced his craft first with short stories on the pages of the pulp magazines of the 1920s and '30s.

It was many years later that he was talked into spinning a yarn for students. *Gentle Ben* was born, and with that story, a new career for the prolific Morey. Though young people became his primary audience, adults also enjoyed his vivid prose. In the last quarter century of his life, he penned sixteen more successful novels. Walt and his books received many awards and honors.

Walt Morey wrote right up to his death in 1992, just weeks before his 85th birthday. His legacy to us all is to be found between the covers of his books.

Colophon

The overall design of this book, and the others in the Walt Morey Adventure Library, was under the direction of Dennis and Linny Stovall of Blue Heron Publishing, Inc.

The cover design is by Judy Quinn of L.grafix in Portland, Oregon. The cover art is by Fredrika Spillman of Mulino, Oregon.

Type in the body of the book is Palatino and Optima, digital typefaces by Adobe Systems Inc., set with a Linotronic Imagesetter and printed on pH-balanced paper in the United States.